Dante's Angels

Dante's Angels

A Novel
by
Diana Kay Lubarsky

Cover design by Sarah Rikaz
www.SarahRikazCreative.com

TOLIFE...Ink
Buffalo N.Y.
Write The Book You Want To Read

Printed in the United States of America

ISBN #: 978-1-387-94288-6

Main category of the book—Novel

First Edition

Contact Information:

Dianakay550@gmail.com

TOLIFE...Ink
Buffalo NY
Write The Book You Want To Read

Some friendships are life rafts
Sustaining us through dark hours
And turbulent waters

Words need not be said
I know you will be there
In my hour of need
As will I for you

Other friendships are sailboats
Navigating us to sunny places
New horizons and adventures

This book is dedicated to
All of my friends
Past, present, and future
You are all Blessings in my life

And the truth is …
I could never have made this journey
Without you

Chapters	Page

CHAPTER 1 —ROGER AND DESMOND

Desmond walked out of the kitchen, a semi-deflated chef's hat sliding over his left eye, olive skin glistening with sweat. He went behind the counter, stood in front of the air-conditioning vent and mopped his brow with a greasy dishtowel. Then he poured himself a glass of ice water and lumbered over to Roger who was standing behind the antique cash register.

"Your old ladies back again?"

"Yep. Every Wednesday morning, like clockwork."

Desmond took a long drink and refilled the glass. "I should have known."

"What do you mean?"

"You're smiling, man. Whenever the five of them show up, you smile. I was just wondering what you see when you look at them."

Roger grinned, wiping down the counter. "I don't know. I guess they remind me of my mom."

"Yeah, well, don't let your mom hear that. Moms don't like to be replaced."

Roger began filling the salt and pepper shakers. "Nah. Can't happen. My mom passed away five years ago. She lived in Florida, and I didn't get to see her very often. When these gals show up—I don't know—it makes me feel like a part of her is still with me."

Desmond dried his hands on his *Goose the Cook* apron and stared across the room at the ladies. "My family all live in the Philippines. I haven't seen my mom in years." He sighed. "I think of her a lot, but there never seems to be a good time to call."

Roger tilted his head, eyebrows raised.

Desmond shuffled his feet. "Time zones, life, it all seems to get in the way. You know how it is."

"Yeah," Roger said quietly. "I know how it is. But if I had the chance to do it over again, I would have made the time." He paused. "Do you want me to introduce you to the ladies?"

Desmond shook his head, '*no*'.

"Well, for what it's worth, they like you."

Desmond's eyes widened and he broke into a grin that lit his face. "How could they like me? They've never even met me for one minute of their lives!"

"Yeah, well, in the four months you've been here, they haven't sent back a single breakfast order. Before you came, with Randolph, I'd say that two out of every three meals went back for some kind of misdemeanor. And Estelle, the little one with white

2

hair, just loves your crescent rolls. In case you haven't noticed, she keeps sneaking batches of them into her pocket book when she thinks we aren't looking."

"Cool." Desmond laughed and headed back into the kitchen. "I hope they keep coming then," he called over his shoulder.

Roger took care of several other customers before returning to refill the ladies' coffee mugs. He wondered what twist their conversation had taken in the last ten minutes. He approached quietly. Ruth was talking.

"They've put me in a 'mommy box,'" Ruth explained.

"A what?"

"A 'mommy box.' Maybe I should have said a 'mom box.' Yes. That sounds better."

Helen scratched her head. "Like a coffin, you mean?"

"No." Ruth shook her head and pushed her breakfast plate away, the food only half-eaten. "It's more of a psychological designation."

Estelle burped. "Excuse me."

Ruth remained silent.

"C'mon, Ruthie," Helen encouraged. "Is this about your kids again?"

Ruth fidgeted with her napkin. "Yeah. I'm thinking that maybe I expect too much of them."

"They're grown-ups, Ruth, you've got to let them go," Helen insisted.

"Speaking of going, I think I have to go again," said Estelle.

She placed a single dollar bill in her pocket to purchase a lottery ticket, then hoisted herself out of her chair and made a beeline for the restroom.

"I know that," Ruth answered emphatically, with raised eyebrows and a forlorn expression.

Bella blew her nose and crunched up the tissue, adding it to the pile of others she had stacked in front of her like a lop-sided mound of snowballs.

"So, what exactly do you want from your kids?"

"I want them to see me as a person, not just their mom. And I want them to like me. And cherish me. And seek me out for advice. And invite me over when they have other company. And help me clean my carpet. And answer all my computer questions. And ..."

"Stop!" cried Ginger, throwing her hands up and knocking over the maple syrup. "Give me a minute to finish my pancakes and get my social worker hat on. I can tell you're going to need a serious reality adjustment today."

Roger walked back toward the kitchen just as Desmond came through carrying a tray of food, which he quickly handed off to another server before passing Roger a basket of freshly baked crescent rolls.

"Now that you told me the little one seems especially fond of them, I made a new batch."

Roger smiled. "I'm sure Estelle will appreciate it."

"Tell her I can bake some for her whenever she's in the neighborhood."

"I will, but I don't think any of them really live around here. From what I've heard, this is a sort of middle meeting ground so that none of them have to travel very far."

Desmond's lips curled into his easy smile again. "And they picked Dante's because of its fine reputation?"

"No," answered Roger. "They picked Dante's because this is where Helen landed the day she crashed her car into the side of our building."

Desmond laughed. "You're kidding, right?"

"Nope. Believe me, I couldn't have made that day up if I tried."

"Which one is Helen?" Desmond asked.

Roger pointed. "The one with the dark-brown hair."

"And she really crashed into the place?"

"Yes, she did. Misjudged the corner. Drove her car straight onto the sidewalk, plowed into the fire hydrant out front, and landed right on our front step."

"Was she hurt?"

"Miraculously, no."

Desmond shook his head. "You saw it all?"

"Not exactly. We'd just finished the breakfast rush when we heard the crash out front and we went running … and there was this red 1993 Chevy Impala, impaled on the top of the hydrant with water shooting *everywhere*."

"And Helen?"

"Still in the car. Me and a few other guys managed to pry the doors open and pull her out. She was walking and talking and didn't seem hurt, so we brought her in here and sat her down at an empty table."

"And then?"

"It was nuts, man. We had to call the fire department, the water department, and the cops ..."

"And Helen?"

"Helen," Roger chuckled, "just leaned back in her chair and asked to see a menu. Cool as a cucumber. Like nothing out of the ordinary had ever happened. We're mopping the floors in the front entrance, and she's ordering Eggs Benedict, a side of fruit salad, and a cup of coffee."

"You remember the order? That's crazy, man,"

"Yep, it sure was. And she ate every crumb of it, too, even while answering the questions of two state troopers and arranging for a tow truck. It was amazing to watch. In seconds, she had those cops wrapped around her little finger. They even paid her bill and drove her home."

"And the rest of the angels came ... when?"

"Angels?" Roger's eyebrows and shoulders shrugged simultaneously.

"We Filipinos believe strongly in angels, don't you know. Anyone who could survive that and not be hurt must surely be one."

"Well … maybe she is. Who knows, maybe they all are," Roger chuckled, scratching his head. "Business definitely picked up after they started coming, especially Wednesday mornings. People seem to like hearing them laugh."

Desmond gave him a big, toothy, *see I told you so* look. "So, how soon after Helen's accident did the rest of them bounce onto the front step?"

Roger smiled as he folded a batch of clean dishtowels. "Apparently, Helen called them all that same night, because the next morning, 9:00 a.m., here they were."

"On top of the fire hydrant?"

"Surprisingly, they actually found their way into the parking lot without running over each other. That was almost two years ago. What can I say? The six of them have been coming here ever since, 9:00 a.m. every Wednesday morning. You can set your watch by them."

"Unbelievable!" Desmond laughed. "Sounds like a group of angels my mom might very much enjoy. And now that you've got me thinking how long it's been since I've spoken to her, I'd best be telephoning her tonight just to check in."

Roger grinned. "Good idea."

Just before disappearing into the kitchen, Desmond called over his shoulder, "Someday I am going to let you introduce me to your angels. And then you are going to have to tell me why you keep saying there are six of them. I've only ever counted five."

Roger turned to the old women in the west corner and listened to the current conversation. The new topic was belly button lint: how to retrieve it, the spectrum of colors it might come in, and any useful purpose it might serve. He bit his lip to keep from laughing out loud, and then followed Desmond into the kitchen.

"Hey, that's right! You haven't met Josie yet. I've got to tell you about Josie, the sixth lady who hasn't been here for a while. Now she was funny!"

CHAPTER 2—DANTE'S CAFÉ

The old ladies pushed two square tables together, dragged their chairs in close and began to whisper. Within minutes their unfiltered conversations and unhinged laughter rocked the entire west corner of the small diner.

Roger swung by, menus in hand, an easy smile rolling across his face. "What's up ladies?"

They took one look at him and inexplicably exploded into another round of laughter. In-between bouts of hysterics, they dabbed their eyes with coffee stained napkins, faces flushed under mops of hair: grayish-silver, salt and pepper, one mahogany red, another deathly brown—all crowning pale skin flecked with age spots they called granny freckles.

Dante's Café was the one place where they felt free to discuss the challenges and anguish of growing old without explanation or criticism. No matter what harsh realities life threw at them, Wednesday morning was always just a few days away, and best friends were sure to make it better.

"So where is the rest of the crew this morning?" asked Roger as he wrote down their breakfast orders.

"Well, Josie had an appointment to get her car serviced," answered Estelle, slipping a dozen little packets of orange marmalade into her purse, along with three onion rolls and two sealed pods of butter. "And Helen ... I don't really know where Helen is. She really should have been here by now... I hope nothing is wrong."

CHAPTER 3 —KISSINGER

Helen arrived late. A half hour late. She burst through the door totally disheveled; red lipstick smudged on her front teeth, dark-brown hair uncombed, mismatched shoes. Plopping into the nearest chair, Helen dropped her purse on the floor and stared at her friends.

"None of you will ever love me again," she wailed. "I'm a murderer!"

Four pair of eyes stared at her.

"What?"

"I killed Kissinger!"

Thirty seconds of silence followed.

Bella spoke first. "Honey, Henry Kissinger died a long time ago."

"Really?" whispered Ruth, fidgeting with her earrings. "I thought he was still alive."

"It doesn't matter whether he's dead or alive. He's old," added Estelle.

"Well, if he died a long time ago, Helen couldn't have killed him. And if he's alive, she didn't do a very good job." Ginger stated. "Either way, dear, you're in the clear, so why don't you just tell us what happened while I look up Kissinger on Google. We'll find out in a minute if he is dead or alive." She rummaged through her purse, found her iPhone, and began punching buttons. "My daughter showed me how to work this damn thing yesterday. If I can only remember."

"It wasn't *Henry* Kissinger!" Helen wailed. "It was Tweety-bird Kissinger."

Ginger put down her iPhone.

Estelle fumbled with her hearing aid.

"My canary!" Helen shrieked. "I vacuumed him. It was an accident! I swear!"

The silence lasted a full five seconds before their shock turned into outright laughter.

"Now, let me get this straight. You have a canary named Kissinger?" Ruth said, coughing up a bite of crusty breadstick.

"Had..." interrupted Helen. "He died."

"In the vacuum cleaner?"

"Yes. And it's not funny!" Helen cried, bouncing between tears and giggles. "He was a good little bird!"

"This I've got to hear." Ruth blew her nose, stuffed the used tissue into the cuff of her left sleeve, and leaned back in her chair.

"Well, my two sons, their wives, and the six grandkids were coming over to our house for dinner last night. I worked all day cleaning and cooking, and by five o'clock I was exhausted. Meanwhile, the stew was burning, the phone kept ringing, I cut my finger slicing the tomatoes, and then I tripped over the damn vacuum cleaner. That's when Kissinger got loose. He flew up to the cornice in the living room and wouldn't come down. He's usually so good when I call, but not last night. I called and called, but he wouldn't come. I felt myself getting angrier and angrier at that damn bird. And that's when it happened."

"What happened?" they shouted.

"Kissinger flew down off the cornice, circled around me once, and shit on my head. I was so furious that I just grabbed that damn vacuum cleaner, aimed … and the next thing I heard was this loud *THWAT* sound … and Kissinger was gone!"

"You vacuumed Kissinger?" the ladies screeched in unison.

"Yes, I did. Stupid bird. It took a few seconds before I realized what I'd done. I hoisted the vacuum up as fast as I could, ripped the canister open, and there lay Kissinger, on his back, with his feet curled up under him, dead as a doornail. And of course just at that very second the front door burst open and all the grandkids charged into the living room yelling, 'Hi, Grammy!'

Lucy and Emma and all the rest of them took one look at Kissinger, dead in the vacuum cleaner, and they ran out of the room, screaming their heads off. It took more than a half hour to calm them all down. I felt just awful. I tried to act nonchalant for the sake of the children, but my heart was racing, and I thought I was going to throw up. Thank God Bill came to the rescue. He picked up Kissinger and put him in the garage so we could bury him after everyone left."

"Oh, honey," said Ginger stroking Helen's shoulder, "losing a pet is hard anytime, but that's taking it to a whole new level."

"Oh, it got much worse after that. Halfway through dinner, Keith announced that he and Lindsay were getting a divorce, he was gay, and this fellow he's been hanging out with lately is his new partner. If I didn't pass out at that moment, I swear I never will." She sighed. "And quite frankly, that's all I remember about the entire evening."

"Wow," murmured the group.

After a brief pause, Helen continued. "I mean we knew something was wrong with their marriage. Lindsay has been so difficult these last two years. We never guessed why. His announcement last night really rocked our foundation. It's going to take a while to process. Made me wonder if I really know anything about anyone. Even my own son."

They all nodded, thoughts turning inward to their own families.

"Kids. You conceive them, grow them, give birth to them, and raise them with all the love you possess. You change your world so that it revolves around them. You do everything for them. They become your center. And then one day you look up and they are gone, and in their place are these grown people. They look like your own children, but their lives are a mystery to you. They have secrets … lots of secrets, and you realize you know nothing at all about these strangers standing in front of you. How does that happen?"

"Did you ever suspect?" Ginger whispered, trying to remember in all her years as a social worker, how many of these conversations she had been a part of.

"If I can be dirt honest, I think I might have. But it was just one of those thoughts that flits through your mind, and then you let it go and think, nah, couldn't be. After all, he has a wife and two kids."

"How's Bill taking it?" asked Ruth.

"Not well. He looked like a bomb went off inside of him, but he didn't say a word. When Bill gets upset, he just turns his feelings in and grits his teeth. After everyone left, he buried Kissinger in the backyard and then went straight to bed. Refused to talk to me. Same thing this morning."

"It's going to be all right," said Estelle. "There are a couple of ladies living three doors down from me. They are so warm and friendly. It's not how it used to be, you know. Nowadays it's okay to be gay. And you still have all the grandkids, so you've got the best of both worlds. And if you need any more inspiration, just think of Maureen O'Hara."

"Maureen O'Hara?"

"Anderson Cooper's mother. I mean, he's so cute, and she must be so proud of him."

Ruth's eyebrows knit together.

"I think you mean Gloria Vanderbilt."

"Vanderbilt, O'Hara, what's the difference? He's adorable. I watch him every night on the television." Estelle smiled and reached out to clasp Helen's hand. "You, Bill, and Keith will be just fine."

"Thanks, sweetie," Helen smiled sorrowfully.

Just then Roger passed by in his crisp white shirt, flashing one of his bright smiles. "Well, ladies, is there anything else I can get for you today?" he asked, topping off their coffees.

"Yes," said Ginger, waving her hand. "Helen came late. She still needs to order her breakfast."

Roger quickly wrote down Helen's order, and headed back to the kitchen.

Ginger glanced across the table at her friend's sad face. After only a moment's hesitation, she spoke. "Ladies, before we do anything else today, I think we ought to make a toast to Kissinger."

"Oh," sniffled Helen, "that would be so nice."

"To Kissinger!" the group energetically yelled, spontaneously raising their water tumblers overhead.

The sound of breaking glass permeated the entire diner as all five glasses collided over the center of the table. Roger took one look at the ladies, dropped his pad and pencil, and ran for the mop.

CHAPTER 4 —ESTELLE

The telephone rang three times before Ruth cleared her throat and managed to croak a raspy, "Hello."

"Ruthie?"

"Yes. Estelle? Is that you?"

"Uh-huh … I didn't wake you, did I?"

"Of course not, it's almost 8:00 o'clock. I was just putting my shoes on. I'll be leaving here as soon as I get Gordon's breakfast together. You're coming, aren't you?"

"I'm not sure if I can."

"Why not?"

"I can't drive this morning. I was wondering if you might be able to pick me up and I could go with you … if it's not too much trouble. Otherwise I won't be able to make it, and I do hate to miss our mornings at Dante's."

"It's no trouble at all," said Ruth, running a comb through her hair. "Is something wrong with your car?"

"Nope. It's not the car. It's me."

"What happened to you?"

Ruth draped a blue silk scarf around her neck.

"Well, you know how David always leaves his stuff around the house. I've been yelling at that man to put his crap away for fifty years. You think he ever listens? Of course not! He still believes what his mother said when she called me his maid. I dunno. Maybe she was right. I have been..."

Ruth interrupted. "Estelle, what happened?"

"I fell. I tripped over his damn shoes on my way to the bathroom Monday night. I called my daughter, Alice. She came over and drove me to the hospital. We were in the emergency room for hours, and they said I cracked my right arm in two places. I have a cast, and a sling, and I won't be able to drive for at least six weeks." Estelle sighed heavily.

"Oh dear, I am so sorry to hear that! You just stay put. I'll be on my way just as soon as I can."

"Thank you so much. But before you hang up, I have one more little favor to ask. Would you mind coming inside for just a minute? I need just a tiny bit of help getting ready. If it's not too much trouble, that is."

"Don't be silly. That's what friends are for," said Ruth, putting on her earrings and pouring pulp-free orange juice into a brandy snifter. "Just tell me what you need."

"Well, I can't seem to tie my shoelaces with my fingers all swollen."

"Don't worry about that for a single second, Estelle. I'll get them tied nice and tight for you." Ruth smiled, reached for a box of corn flakes, and was about to hang up when Estelle continued talking.

"And the dog food."

"What?"

"I can't open the can of dog food."

"Oh. Sorry. We don't have any animals, so I keep forgetting that other people do," said Ruth, putting a paper filter into the coffee pot and filling the base with water. "It's okay. I'll get the can open and feed the beast."

"He's not a beast," Estelle protested. "He's a Chihuahua. His name is Morton. Named for my great-grandfather, Morton Morris Lieberman … on my mother's side, you know."

Ruth sighed. "Just get yourself together, Estelle, and I will be over in about twenty minutes. I will tie your shoes, open the can of dog food, and feed Morton. And then we will go off to Dante's. Okay?"

"But what about Gloria?"

"Gloria? Who's Gloria?

"Remember, I told you about her last week. She's my new rescue Chihuahua. She's a girl. And she needs a different kind of food."

Ruth took a deep breath. She remembered what she heard once on the Dr. Oz show, about how smiling makes your endorphins shine, or something like that. She forced her lips to curl upward and made a pleasant face.

"Of course, we will feed Gloria also," she said in her most

cheerful voice. "Anything else?"

Estelle propped her phone against the porcelain rooster that decorated her kitchen table and, using her left hand, proceeded to remove three pink plastic curlers from above each ear. As she twirled her snow-white hair into little ringlets, she looked down. Daisy, her large gray cat, had begun to lick her toes. "Uh … nothing else I can think of at this moment," she said nervously. "Oh, and I'll leave the front door unlocked, so you don't have to ring the bell. David is still sleeping, and I wouldn't want to disturb him. This has been very hard on him, you know. We had to order out the last few days because I couldn't cook."

"Hrumff," Ruth mumbled through gritted teeth. Ruth hung up the phone, put a bowl of fruit salad and a container of 2% milk on the table, and went into the bedroom. She poked Gordon in the ribs.

"Get up, lazy bones," she said, grabbing her purse. "Your breakfast is on the table and I'm leaving."

CHAPTER 5—BELLA AND BOJO

"I can't believe they're going to name the baby Bojo. Bojo Griffin Spindleman." Bella swallowed hard and looked at her friends. Her face was as gray as her hair. "What am I supposed to do?" She was nearly in tears.

"You'll love the child. That's what you'll do," answered Ruth in her professional nurse-in-charge voice. "Here, have some hand sanitizer," she added, passing around a small bottle filled with thick, clear fluid. "It's cold season, you know."

Ignoring the hand sanitizer, Helen began pouring maple syrup on her pancakes. "Is Bojo a boy or a girl?"

"A boy. I think. You know, I don't really trust those home tests, but Bonnie and Joe seem to have faith in them. They scream if I even look at anything pink." Bella reached into her purse and pulled out two beautiful pink hair ribbons. Then, with a sheepish grin, quickly shoved them into the pocket of her gray overcoat.

Estelle sat quietly on her side of the table. The cast on her right arm was covered with signatures and decals. Seemingly oblivious of the conversation around her, she was busily trying to decide which herbal tea to choose from the large assortment Roger had placed beside her. She picked up one packet labeled Mint Julep and tore open the outer envelope with her teeth.

Bella hung her head. "Bojo. My God. What will they think of next?" She began to hiccup. "What is wrong with kids these days? Whatever happened to names like Sam or Jane? Why do they have to go making things up, like Bojo?" she wailed.

"Shush, Bella." Indoor voice, remember? Everyone is staring at you," scolded Helen.

"I don't care," Bella screeched. "I worked in a library for twenty years, and all I ever did was whisper. Now that I'm finally retired, I can yell as loud as I want." She blew her nose noisily, scrunched up the tissue, and threw it on the table.

Helen shrugged and began cutting her pancakes into neat little squares. "You know, it could be worse," she said, lining up each square according to size. "I heard Josie's daughter named her twins Pilot and Skye."

"You're kidding."

"Nope. Pilot is the boy, and Skye is the girl. Her daughter-and son-in-law travel a lot and thought it was cute."

"Well, they could have named them Madagascar and Bermuda, I suppose," mumbled Ruth.

Estelle took the straw out of her water glass and used it to brush Bella's crumpled tissue onto the floor; then she carefully lifted her teacup with her left hand and looked around. "Say, where is Josie, anyhow? Didn't she say she'd be here this week?"

"She and Arthur are touring Italy with the Steinbergs,"

responded Ruth and Ginger simultaneously.

"Really?"

"That's a great trip. When are they due back?" asked Helen.

"About two weeks, I think." Ruth put away her bottle of hand sanitizer and began wiping down the salt and pepper shakers with floral-scented hand wipes.

The conversation stalled as Roger approached with coffee and tea refills. Between bites of scrambled eggs, Bella started up again.

"There are some really wonderful babies naming books at the library. I was thinking that maybe I ought to drop one of them off at their house. You know, one with normal baby names. What do you all think? I mean, the baby is not due for another three months. Maybe if they saw some good alternatives, they would change their minds."

Ruth waved a piece of crispy bacon around as if it were a baton. "Give it up Bella; you don't have a prayer. All you're going to do is alienate your daughter and son-in-law. Shut your mouth, and when the baby is born and looks up at you and coos, it won't matter if his name is Hasenpfeffer. You'll love him."

"You really think so?" Bella sobbed.

"Yes," added Helen. "And believe me, I know how hard that is. I mean, keeping your mouth shut. And if you think it's hard talking to your daughter, just try talking to your daughter-in-law. Get her mad and you'll never see your son again, or the grandkids." She took a bite of her omelet. "These eggs seem a little bland today. Estelle, could you pass the salt and pepper?"

Estelle looked up. "How'd they come up with Bojo anyhow?" She handed Helen a bottle of ketchup.

"It's *Bonnie* and *Joe* smushed together. They decided the baby's name should reflect their union. Yuck! That's what I think. You know, someone ought to write a book on how to be a parent to an adult child. It's a lot harder than I ever thought it would be. They really think they're so much smarter than we are, and they're not. They have no idea what the hell they're doing."

"Salt and pepper, please," Helen shouted again, this time into Estelle's left ear.

Ruth shook her head from side to side. "Aw, come on. Be honest now, Bella. When you were twenty-eight did your parents know anything? I mean, how many kids did you have at twenty-eight?"

"Three, with one on the way. And my folks always hated Aldon. They thought he was stuck up and the match wouldn't work." Bella buttered a large chunk of bagel and stuffed it into her mouth. When she started to speak, a half dozen little bits of mushed bread flew like projectiles across the table. "The truth is, there are days I can kill him. But after forty-nine years, I'm beginning to think we just might make it." She wiped her lips with a crinkled napkin and took another bite.

Helen stood, reached over Estelle, and grabbed the salt and pepper shakers.

Ginger suddenly began to cry.

"What's wrong, sweetie?" asked Helen.

Ginger continued to sob. Tears blurred her mascara and dripped onto her poached eggs.

"You know, this coming May will be two years since my oldest daughter, Leah, passed away from ovarian cancer." She wiped her eyes. Her hands were shaking. "Well, Harry, my son-in-law, called last night to tell us his firm is relocating to Korea for three years. He thinks it would be a really good career move and he is tempted to go with them. Jessica is nine and Scott is only seven. If they move to Korea, I won't see them for three whole years. I didn't think I would survive losing Leah. I just can't lose them, too."

Ginger stared into Bella's face. "You have a new baby coming into your life, Bella. Don't you understand what a blessing that is? Whatever his name is, it doesn't matter a hoot."

Roger brought over a small packet of tissues, refilled the water glasses, and topped off Ginger's coffee for the third time.

When she calmed down, Ginger confronted Bella. "If I can live with the handle of Ginger Esmerelda Rosenberg, your new little guy can make it through with Bojo Griffin Spindleman, and that's a fact! Now shut up about all this nonsense and finish your bagel."

"Ginger Esmerelda Rosenberg? Good grief!" mumbled Helen. "And I thought my name was awful."

Bella began stacking the used dishes one atop the other. Her face became more relaxed and her eyes more hopeful. "Well," she said, "I've got to give it at least one more good try. Just maybe, by next week I'll be able to tell you that Bonnie and Joe changed their minds about the baby's name."

"Good luck with that one," said Ruth, rummaging through her pocketbook for her wallet.

Ginger rubbed her throat. "I think that old hive on my neck has popped up again. Anybody see anything?"

Ruth craned her head forward, her reading glasses propped on the bridge of her nose.

"Well it certainly is a hive."

"Yep, a really big one this time," added Bella, between a bevy of hiccups.

"Probably stress related," added Estelle.

Ginger immediately began applying cortisone cream to the affected area.

"You know, hives are not nearly as significant as hiccups," Bella abruptly announced.

Ginger's face flushed. "Why would you say such a thing?"

"Because my mother once told me that whenever I hiccup it means she's thinking of me. And that is significant. But when you get a hive, it's only because you're a neurotic."

"Well, your mother died 30 years ago so she's no longer thinking of you! And I am not a neurotic," responded Ginger in a screechy voice three octaves above normal.

Before the rest of the group could weigh in, Roger came by

again. "Anyone interested in dessert?" he asked, clearing the breakfast dishes. He smiled at the group with obvious affection.

"I'm going to pass," said Ruth, pushing her seat away from the table. "It's getting late and I promised Gordon I'd be home before noon."

"Yeah. I've gotta get going also," added Ginger, wrapping a paisley scarf around her neck to cover the growing hive. "Will I see you all next week?"

"God willing," answered Estelle.

"Yes. Hopefully, we'll all still be alive by then," added Helen.

"Well, if you're dead stay home," stated Bella. "We'll come visit you after breakfast."

With a shrug and one last chuckle, the five old ladies slowly stood, brushing all unwanted breakfast crumbs onto the floor.

By 11:05 they had gathered their belongings, finished with the bathroom brigade, paid their bills, and were finally ready to go outside.

Roger held the door open while the women, pulling hoods over their heads, exited into the light rain. After another group hug, they climbed in their separate cars, being extra careful not to crash into each other on the way out of the parking lot.

The rain slowed. Rays of sunlight began to spear through the clouds.

On her way home, Bella began to imagine rocking the new baby in her arms. "Bojo," she whispered, trying out the name

"You hear anything they were saying?" Ralph asked with a big grin and a sparkle in his eye.

"Not much. Something about their daughters being wild and swinging loose. Then they switched to baking. Sounded like a lot of reaching and scooping, different sized measuring cups and jelly. Don't know what's so funny about any of that stuff."

"Brassieres," said Ralph.

"What?"

"Brassieres … They're talking about how each of them hoists their tits into brassieres." Ralph laughed. "I never knew lining up both nipples to face the same direction was such a chore."

Ralph took in the startled expression on Roger's face and smiled. "It wasn't their daughters who were wild and loose," he continued. "What you heard them say was their 'girls'… you know … their knockers. That's what's wild and loose. And the bending over, scooping up and measuring…"

"Don't tell me anymore," said Roger, holding up his hands.

"Yep. Not baking cupcakes, that's for sure. Good luck with this crew today," said Ralph with a wink.

"Well, at least it's not dildos," Roger whispered under his breath.

"Nah. Thongs and dildos—that was last week. Shame you missed it. Now that was a real hoot," said Ralph, tipping his hat to the ladies on his way out the door.

CHAPTER 7—ACHES AND PAINS

Ruth dragged herself through the front door of Dante's Café. Her shoulder-length salt-and-pepper hair had been thoroughly tousled by the wind. Estelle, short and round, followed closely behind, a fringe of little white ringlets bouncing out from under her vintage trilby hat with each step. A black eye patch peeked out from under the brim.

"What happened to your eye?" Bella yelled from across the restaurant.

"I'm trying out my pirate costume for Halloween. How does it look?" Estelle shouted back.

"No, seriously, what happened?"

Estelle sat down next to Bella and removed her jacket. "I had a lump under my eyelid and the doctor insisted that it be removed. I just have to wear this dumb patch for a week until the biopsy comes in. Nothing too serious, the doctor says." She shrugged, pushing the trilby lower down on her forehead.

Ginger entered the café five minutes later, leaning heavily on an alpine ski pole and tilting precariously to the left. She gently eased into the chair closest to Estelle.

"Are you all right?" Ruth asked.

"Not really. My back is out." Ginger grimaced, squirming uncomfortably. She carefully rotated her body while trying to find a place to prop up the ski pole. Giving up, she just slid it under the table.

"Ow!" cried Estelle.

"Sorry, dear," Ginger said, kicking the ski pole in a different direction.

Ruth pulled the pole out from under the table and dragged it across the room, wedging it upright in the nearest corner. Then she shuffled back to her seat.

"I signed up for a Pilates course last week, and halfway through the first session something popped," said Ginger, staring at Estelle's eye patch.

"Well, then, I guess me and my bum foot came to the right place today," Bella announced.

They all looked under the table. Bella's foot was in a bright-blue orthopedic boot.

"Good grief! So, what's your story?"

"Aldon, again. That is, his feet. I mean I tripped over Aldon's feet and broke two toes."

She blew her nose in a tissue and threw it across the table. "A few months ago Estelle tripped over David's shoes, and a few days ago I tripped over Aldon's feet. What can I say?"

"Hmm," murmured Ginger, taking a clean napkin and brushing Bella's used tissue onto the floor. "Our men are never too old to cause trouble."

"I'll second that," Ruth murmured. Her eyes were bloodshot and her face pale. She scrutinized her friends. "We really do look like a collection of broken toys, don't we?" Then, twisting her head around, she scanned the area and added, "By the way, where's Helen?"

"At the doctor's," said Ginger. "She called me this morning. Her cold turned into bronchitis."

"And Josie?"

"Who knows," said Bella, shifting her weight, trying to lift her foot so it could rest on the empty chair. "She and Arthur have some kind of appointment. I don't remember what. Said she'd see us next week."

Ruth propped her head in her hands and closed her eyes.

"Okay, Ruthie, what's wrong with you?" asked Ginger. "Are you sick, also?"

"No. Just very tired. Gordon sliced the top of his head open Sunday morning. It took fifteen stitches to close the gash."

The group gasped. "Is he okay?"

"Oh yeah. He's fine ... home now, a wounded warrior who can't even make himself a cup of tea. 'Ruth, can you get me this,' and 'Ruth, can you get me that?' I've been on nursemaid duty for the last four days, and I'm exhausted. I don't think I worked this hard when I was in charge of the entire surgical wing at Jarvis Medical Center back home." Ruth stopped to take a sip of coffee and absentmindedly shoved her half-eaten dinner roll into her purse. "But it wasn't until he woke me up in the middle of the night to scratch his back that I found myself plotting to murder him." She slumped and lowered her head onto the table. "I just haven't decided whether to do it before or after his stitches are removed."

"I think you should wait until after," Estelle advised. "It may be hard to explain to the doctor why he has to remove stitches from a dead guy."

"Definitely after." Ginger nodded, sipping her coffee. "Is there anything we can do to help?"

"Nope. We're fine. Fortunately, he's got a very hard head."

"How the hell did he manage to crack his head open?" asked Bella. "Was he in a car accident?"

"No. But what did happen is so incredibly stupid that I'm embarrassed to say it out loud."

"Oh, goodie!" Bella squealed, rubbing her hands together. "I love other people's stupid stuff."

"Well, you're not going to believe this one," Ruth teased. She looked at her friends with wide eyes. A mischievous grin crawled across her face. "It all started when Gordon and I woke up late Sunday morning and began fooling around."

"And you sliced his head open for that? Was he performing that badly?" Bella giggled.

"No! Now be quiet or I won't tell you!"

"Okay, so you were fooling around, lucky girl...and?"

"And afterward, he got up and said, 'Honey, I'm gonna go jump into the shower now.' And feeling kind of goofy, I said that I wanted to watch him jump into the shower. So, with this really serious expression on his face, the idiot yanked off his pajamas, strutted his stark naked self to the furthest corner of our bedroom, spun around and ran, full speed, toward the bathroom. He had just managed to clear the threshold with a sort of flying leap, when at the last minute, he turned to wave at me. Needless to say, the jerk missed the shower door and instead smacked his head up into the sharp metal bar on top of the stall. He crashed. I caught him. The rest is history."

"Geez Louise!" yelled Bella so loudly that her foot fell off the chair.

Ruth took a sip of water and continued.

"Aside from being incredibly funny, it was also pretty gruesome. The whole top of his head split open, and he was bleeding all down his face and all over my pink nightie. I felt like Jacqueline Kennedy in her bloody pink suit."

"What a horrible image." Ginger cringed while helping prop Bella's foot up again.

"Did he lose consciousness?" asked Estelle.

"No. Thank goodness. But it looked awful. I told him we needed to get to the emergency room, fast, but the idiot wouldn't listen. He insisted on taking a shower first. I dressed quickly and threatened to go to the hospital without him if he didn't get some pants on immediately. Eventually, he got dressed, and off we went.

It wasn't until we were halfway there that his head started really throbbing and he slumped down in his seat."

The rest of the ladies were staring at Ruth with open mouths.

"The folks in the emergency room took him back right away," Ruth continued. "I guess it was all that blood. But they wouldn't let me in with him, despite my professional credentials. Still, I could pinpoint the minute they asked how he sliced his head open, because you could hear them laughing all the way down the corridor." Ruth took another deep breath. "God, I'm tired," she whined.

"Me, too," sighed Bella.

Ginger kept twisting around in her chair, trying to find a comfortable spot. "And I hurt all over," she moaned. "The hell with the fifty dollars I prepaid. No more Pilates for me. It's a young woman's sport. I wish I could do it, I really do, and maybe a few years ago I could have. But now, I just can't."

"Wise decision, lady."

"You know, I never gave my body permission to get old," Ginger lamented.

"None of us ever did, dear," said Ruth. "Do you know how long it took me to figure out that old people walk funny because they are in pain? Who knew?"

Estelle adjusted the patch on her eye. "Remember, these are the 'golden years.' "

"God, how I hate that expression!" Ruth grumbled. "I don't find it at all amusing. In fact, it makes me downright angry. Every time someone says, 'So they call these the golden years,' I feel like picking up a baseball bat and bashing them in the head."

Roger came over to the table and placed a menu in front of each woman. "Anyone else coming today ladies?"

"Not today Roger. It's just the four of us. And we're all miserable. Any menu specials to make us feel better?" asked Estelle, slipping him a dollar for her weekly lottery ticket.

After a brief discussion, the ladies unanimously accepted Roger's suggestions. Dry English muffins and decaf coffees were replaced with generous slices of Black Forest cake topped with mountains of whipped cream and large glasses of wine.

No one seemed at all interested in going home that morning, and the ladies stayed at Dante's until well after noon, telling stupid husband stories and laughing their heads off.

CHAPTER 8—MIRACLE CURES

"Miracle-Cures," said Helen, reading the label on the brown bottle in Bella's hand. "Is that one word or two separate words? I mean, first of all there are miracles, and then there are cures. Either way, it all sounds rather hokey to me."

Bella kept rubbing the cramp in her right calf. "Oh, stop being such a fuddy-duddy. The information packet that came with it says this bottle is only the first of 500 miracle cures easily purchased from Healyoursymptoms.com. It's only $15.99 for a one-ounce bottle or $25.99 for two. A bargain!" She began to apply the lotion.

"Oh my God!" Ruth held her nose. Her eyes began to water. "It smells like doggy doo. What's in it?"

Bella stopped applying the lotion, lifted the bottle, and began searching the label for an ingredient list. There was none. Meanwhile, the horrendous odor permeated the air, drifting like smoke on a lazy afternoon breeze. Her friends began covering their faces with any available napkin or handkerchief as they pushed their chairs away from both the table and Bella. Estelle's napkin fell to the floor. While bending over to retrieve it, she happened to glanced at Bella's leg.

"Bella!" Estelle cried in alarm, "Your whole leg is turning bright orange!"

Bella looked down at her right leg. Not only was it orange, but it was beginning to burn. Bella jumped out of her seat and made a beeline for the ladies' room. Ruth ran after her. Helen got up and sprayed their area of the dining room with a canister of air sanitizer she'd found in Ruth's purple tote.

Five minutes passed.

A flustered Bella emerged from the bathroom. Her right leg was no longer bright orange, but rather a rosy pink. She walked slowly back toward the table. All of her friends stared at her.

"What?" she challenged.

"How are you feeling?" asked Estelle.

"Fine," she replied. "See, I told you this stuff would work. The leg cramps are all gone." She smiled, stuffed the bottle of Miracle-Cures back into its brown paper bag, and continued eating her breakfast. When nobody was looking she casually shoved the bag under a nearby table where she conveniently forgot it when the group left Dante's an hour later.

CHAPTER 9—RUTH'S JOURNAL #1

Ruth stared at the blank paper.

"I don't know how I'm supposed to do this?" she thought out loud.

Gordon looked up from behind his newspaper. "What are you trying to do?"

"I joined a writing group last week. I'm supposed to have one or two pages done by Thursday, and I just can't think of anything to write."

"Well, what's important to you?"

"I dunno. You and the kids, I guess. But I really don't feel like writing about us."

"How about something on your breakfast club?"

Ruth swiveled back and forth in her office chair while chewing the nail on her right index finger.

"I guess I could write about how we all met. That's kind of a funny story."

"Sounds good."

Gordon's head was back in the newspaper; he was gone. Still, it was a plausible idea. She picked up her pen and began to write.

Writing Class Essay:

~~Dear Class~~ ~~Dear Abby~~ ~~First Draft~~ ~~My Story~~

Ruth's Journal #1

Three years ago, me and my husband Gordon sold our home of 35 years and moved to Oregon. We had lived in New York all our lives. But we needed family and ours had all grown, leaving our house empty of noise and fingerprints. Our youngest daughter and her husband moved to Portland the year before and begged us to follow. After much reflection, we did.

At first we thought we would be happy. But once all the hard work of moving and setting up was done, we realized how much we missed the friends we had left behind. Holidays came and went, yet seemed empty. Being with Lillian and Richard and the kids once a week was wonderful, just not enough.

Back in New York, the synagogue was the center of our spiritual and social life. Most of our friends had come from this source.

After some thought, we joined a synagogue in the Portland area. It wasn't long before the social director sent around a flyer asking who would be interested in joining a new Havurah for seniors. A Havurah is like a friendship circle. Well, Gordon and I were certainly seniors, and in need of friends, so we signed on.

Seventeen couples showed up at the first meeting. Wow. What a crew. We were all seniors, for sure, but with vast differences. Those at the younger end were still in their 50s, working, some with kids still at home. Quite a lively bunch. And then there were others. Eighties and nineties: canes, crutches, oxygen tanks, and wheelchairs. Nice people, but, "What did you say! Speak louder, my hearing aid died." Yes. We were different.

We decided to meet once a month, alternating houses. Four weeks later, the host seemed relieved when only fourteen couples actually showed up. Time passed and we were down to twelve couples, then ten, and by spring only six couples were still involved.

That last meeting in June is when my world changed. It's when the six women in the kitchen took a good hard look at the six men in the living room and decided to permanently kick all the guys out of the Havurah.

That was two years ago. It was the beginning of our breakfast club, and the close friendships that changed Oregon from a West Coast state, to my home.

The End.

By Ruth Sussman

Ruth read her essay several times and was quite pleased. After only a few minor corrections, she closed her notepad and went to sleep.

CHAPTER 10—CEMETERIES

It was a quarter past ten, and the breakfast rush in Dante's Café was almost over. Roger and Ralph were discussing the latest football scandal when a sudden burst of laughter made them glance toward the ladies in the west corner.

"After all this time, I still get a kick outta hearing the old broads laugh," said Ralph. "They remind me of my mom and her old cronies playing Pinochle back at our bar in Seattle. Man, they could outdrink and out-cuss all the men half their age."

Roger nodded. "The last week or two they seemed so down, I was getting worried. But now the sun finally came out, and they seem cheerful again."

"Nothin' to do with the weather," said Ralph. "With women, it always comes down to money. I just overheard one of them say she spent big bucks and they're all real excited about her buy."

"Which one?"

"Brown hair."

"That's Helen, the retired math teacher. She rechecks all their tabs and counts all the pennies. God help me if I add anything wrong. She'll nail me immediately." Roger smiled. "So what did she buy this time?"

"Burial plots."

"Of course she did," mumbled Roger, shaking his head. He grabbed a large water pitcher from behind the counter and walked into the kitchen.

"Really," said Helen. "We looked all over, and this was the best cemetery deal around. It's well maintained, and they've just opened a brand-new section on a hilltop with a beautiful view of the valley. And," she said, pushing her plate to the side, "by signing up for the early bird special we were allowed first choice of sites." Her mouth widened into a gentle grin.

"My folks always talked about their corner plot with a view of a flower garden," said Ruth, opening a packet of orange marmalade and smearing it across her English muffin. "Of course, that was before they died."

"You haven't heard much from them since, I presume," said Ginger, waving to the couple who just came in.

"No. But I do often wonder if they're enjoying it."

Helen removed a map of the cemetery from her purse and spread it across the table. She pointed to the upper-right-hand corner, which was quickly covered with butter and maple syrup from Estelle's pancakes.

"See? This is where we are."

"Don't be silly. " Estelle sneezed twice. "You're sitting right next to me," she said, wiping her nose.

Ignoring Estelle's comments, Helen continued, "We only bought two plots this time. Back in Minnesota, our family mausoleum was large enough for four. Now that we live in Oregon, I guess we'll have to sell the old plots."

Roger swung by to check on them. Everything seemed all right, so he moved on.

"How do you sell a mausoleum?" asked Bella, stuffing most of a fried egg into her mouth.

"Craigslist, of course," answered Helen, "although it will be hard to let it go. My mom is buried in that cemetery, along with my grandmother, two aunts, and a few cousins. We used to visit them several times a year. Washed the bugs off the tombstones and pulled out encroaching weeds. Never visited my dad nearly as often, mostly because he decided to move with his second wife to Florida. He died on vacation in Hawaii, and we had to ship him all the way cross-country, so he could be buried next to *her*. Did you know it costs more to ship a casket in the hold of a plane than it does if the guy was stuffed into a first-class seat? I swear, next time he travels up front!"

Estelle leaned forward. "And I'm sure he will appreciate every moment of the trip, dear."

"Well, I'm curious about this new cemetery you just chose," said Ruth. "Does it allow you to have a headstone, or only one of those square metal plaques they stick on top of the grass?"

"Unfortunately, this cemetery only allows the metal plaques."

Estelle's brows furrowed. "You know, that means they'll ride over you with the lawn mowers."

"Yes. But it does help keep down the cost of perpetual care."

"And the lawn mowers are very loud," Estelle continued.

Helen looked pensive. "Well, my hearing is not what it used to be, so maybe the mowing won't bother me too much. And I always did love the smell of freshly cut grass."

"I'm allergic to grass," said Estelle, taking all the rolls from the breadbasket, wrapping them in a paper napkin, and stuffing them into her pocketbook. "I'd probably start sneezing in my grave and scare the hell out of everyone." She snorted. "They'll have to bury me with a whole box of tissues if I end up at that place."

"I always wanted to be buried in a Christian cemetery," Bella announced to no one in particular.

"Why?" The group looked up, clearly surprised.

"I love the statues of angels standing on top of the tombstones. I always wanted to have an angel looking down at me, smiling and spreading her wings over my resting place. I find that image so comforting."

"Jewish people are not supposed to have angels on their graves," chided Ruth.

"I know," Bella pouted, "but let's face it, Jewish people are not supposed to eat bacon either. Still, here we are," she said popping the last crispy strip into her mouth.

Helen lifted the cemetery map from the breakfast table. She tried folding it along the creases while inadvertently dripping maple syrup on Ginger's new Coach purse. "Well, I don't eat bacon, or any other kinds of pork," she said, giving up on neatness and smashing the map down any which way so that she could shove it back in her bag.

"And you don't want angels either, I suppose."

"Nope," said Helen.

"Well, sorry about that," Bella continued, cramming a piece of bagel into her mouth with one hand while trying to peel a chunk of dried egg yolk off her chest with the other. "What can I say? I love bacon, and angels."

"So, are you planning to get buried in a Christian cemetery, then?" asked Ginger.

"Nope. No angels. Aldon won't hear of it."

"So, what are you going to do?"

"We've already strolled around the two cemeteries that belong to our synagogue. One has headstones and the other has metal plaques. We'll probably go with the headstones. Sadly, no angels this time around, only a few pebbles on top if we are lucky enough to have any visitors."

"I wonder where Josie and Arthur plan to be buried," said Ginger, rummaging through her purse. "I'm sure she said she was going to be here this morning. By the way, does anyone have a nail file? I seem to have a jagged edge." She held her left thumb up for examination.

Bella reached into her purse, pulled out a five-inch metal file shaped like a dagger and tossed it across the table. It landed in Ginger's plate, impaling her poached egg.

"Bella!" Ginger screeched.

"Sorry," Bella whispered, fidgeting in her chair. "Apparently, Josie had more heart palpitations last night and went running to her cardiologist this morning." Bella shrugged. "She told me she'd be here next week for sure though."

"I hope she's okay," Ruth stated as she turned to the vacated table behind them, grabbed the half-full basket of leftover dinner rolls, and started passing them around to her friends.

"Josie's going to call me this afternoon. I'll let you all know if it's anything serious," Bella said. "But I doubt it."

"Well, getting back to cemeteries, I don't need angels," Ruth continued. "Seeing those little pebbles lined up on top of the headstone will be good enough for me. When we visit the old cemeteries in New York, we're always scouring the grounds for small stones to place on the tombstones of our relatives. We've even placed pebbles on the headstones of the Jewish soldiers in Arlington National Cemetery."

"Did anyone ever place stones on a non-Jewish grave?" asked Estelle.

"I did … once," Ginger reflected. "My old high school chum's daughter, Leslie, died in a terrible car accident two years ago, and was buried in a Christian cemetery. I went with my friend to visit Leslie's grave whenever possible, and we always brought flowers. One day I couldn't get any flowers, so I asked if I could follow the Jewish tradition of placing tiny rocks on top of Leslie's headstone. I explained that in Jewish cemeteries that was our simple way of acknowledging someone had been by to visit. My friend really seemed to like that idea, and the next time I came back, Leslie's tombstone was completely encrusted with beautiful, colorful, precious gems. It was lovely."

"Yes, little stones ..." Ruth leaned back in her chair, ignoring the orange marmalade dripping off her roll. "Rather than getting buried, sometimes I think it would be simpler if Gordon and I just got cremated and had our ashes sprinkled on a mountain top, or in a lake, or something."

"Or flushed down the toilet," added Estelle.

Ruth glared at Estelle.

"Cremation is also forbidden by Jewish law. Why would you want to do that?" asked Ginger.

"Forbidden? Like bacon and angels? Yeah, well, I suppose. But let's face facts," said Ruth, "aside from Lillian and Richard, who live only a few miles away, the rest of our kids and grandkids are spread all over the country. Between the busy lives they lead and the cost of air travel, they hardly ever come to Oregon. If they don't visit us while we're alive, why would they visit us after we're dead? It's sad that families like ours have scattered so far and wide." Ruth's lips quivered, and her eye filled with tears.

Helen leaned forward and clasped Ruth's hand. "Just think about that for a minute, Ruth. Has this generation really changed that much from past generations?" she asked. "My grandparents also left their parents behind. So did yours. But they didn't go to another state—they immigrated to another country. What you're looking for is a family plot. Well, that's just not going to happen. Since World War II there's been no such thing as a family plot for Jews. In today's world, we are a people on the move. Bill and I came to Oregon from Minnesota. You came from New York; Ginger came from New Jersey; Estelle and Bella from California. We all left our parents behind, just as they left their parents behind. And I suppose the reality is that our children will leave us behind as well."

"That is so sad!" said Bella. "To think that no one will ever visit us when we're gone, or put little pebbles on the top of our tombstones."

"Or plaques," interjected Helen.

"Or plaques," Bella conceded.

"I have an idea," said Estelle, eyeing the breadbasket's two remaining crescent rolls. "How about if those of us still standing promise to visit the gravesite of whoever kicks the bucket before us … with pockets full of pebbles?"

"What a sweet idea, said Ginger, an easy smile blooming across her face. "I like that. We could make a tontine, only with little stones."

"What's a tontine?" Estelle whispered to Ruth.

"It's kind of like an agreement, or pact, that the last one standing gets it all." Ruth smiled. "Usually, it's for money, but in our case it could be for pebbles."

"Wonderful," said Helen. "I'm in."

The other ladies all agreed.

"Should we prick our fingers and become blood-brothers first?" asked Estelle.

"Absolutely not!" said Ruth. "Holding hands in a tight circle for a minute will do nicely."

That was exactly what they did, and that was the morning the Dante's Breakfast Club Death Pact was formally founded.

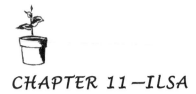

CHAPTER 11—ILSA

Driving like a madwoman, Ruth steered her car into the first parking spot on the left and slammed on the brakes, screeching to a halt only inches from the front door. She stuck her handicapped tag on the rearview mirror and sprinted into Dante's Café. She had overslept by half an hour, but good fortune had prevailed. On the way to Dante's, traffic had been minimal, and she'd sailed through every light on her journey, a number of which were still green or yellow at the time.

Ruth looked around the restaurant. Surprised at being first to arrive, she sucked in three relaxation breaths, as taught by her Silver Sneaker instructor, and began to shove their two square tables together in the west corner. Then she sat down and waited. A tall, blond, waif-like waitress handed her a menu. Ruth smiled, growling under her breath the moment the woman turned away. Where were all the others, she wondered?

Ten minutes ticked by. The waitress came by again, but Ruth would not order. Dante's was getting crowded, people backed up at the entrance, some staring unkindly at Ruth, who remained in tight possession of two tables and six chairs.

On the waitress's third pass, while refusing to order, Ruth asked, "What's your name?"

"Ilsa."

"Ilsa, tell Roger to bring me a coffee. Decaf. On a separate check, please."

"I can get your coffee today, ma'am."

"I'd prefer Roger."

"Roger is not here."

"What do you mean, not here? Is he sick?"

"Roger doesn't work Tuesdays."

There was a long pause.

Ruth placed her hand on her chest, trying to quiet a flurry of palpitations.

"Tuesday?"

"Yes."

"Today?"

"Yes."

"Are you certain?"

"Yes."

Ruth took another three relaxation breaths, squared her shoulders, and in the most dignified manner she could muster, added, "In that case, please make my coffee to go."

CHAPTER 12—GIFTS

"Oh my God!" Bella shrieked. "Somebody has taken our spot. Quick, Ruth, find Roger and tell him!"

Bella glared at their two tables in the west corner, now covered by a very long Zombie Apocalypse tablecloth. She grabbed a corner of the covering and tried to rip it off. With each tug, six wrapped gifts and a small colorful box shifted closer to the edge. Estelle caught the box just before it dropped to the floor.

"Let go of that tablecloth, Bella! It's not yours," Ruth shouted from across the room.

"But these are our tables," Bella protested.

"Well, maybe not today. Now let it go!"

Bella, growling under her breath, let go.

"Oooh. These are birthday candles." Estelle squealed with delight, staring at the little box in her hands for a moment before absentmindedly dropping it into the pocket of her floppy blue sweater.

The main dining area of Dante's was full, as usual, but only a half-dozen people were sitting in the west corner … every one of whom turned to stare when Helen walked across the expanse, yelling "Surprise!" at the top of her lungs. As soon as Helen was in the very center of the room, she took a deep breath, closed her eyes, and began to sing.

"Happy Anniversary to us! Happy Anniversary to us! Happy Anniversary, dear us, Happy Anniversary to us! Yay!"

Then she spun around, ran back into the kitchen and returned seconds later cradling a large bowl of pink whipped cream. Just behind her, carrying a three-layer chocolate cake topped with Fourth of July sparklers was Desmond, a sheepish grin plastered on his face. And bringing up the rear was a laughing Roger juggling two bottles of white wine and half-a-dozen glasses.

Helen straightened the tablecloth as she, Roger, and Desmond put their goodies down. Then she looked up at her friends with delight. The startled women did not react. In fact, they remained frozen in place, like four conjoined ice cubes.

"What in God's name are you doing?" Bella finally asked, breaking the silence.

"Celebrating, of course!" Helen twittered, reaching under the table to retrieve a giant plastic bag with the Target logo.

"Here, take one of these and pass the rest around," she said, handing Bella a stack of pointy cardboard party hats with "#1 Mom" scrawled in floral letters.

Bella examined the hats, snapping the thin rubber chinstraps several times. "And where exactly do you want me to shove these?"

"Oh, Bella!" Helen laughed. "It's a party. Lighten up!" She reached into the Target bag again, and pulled out a stack of blue napkins.

Estelle picked them up. "These say 'Welcome Baby Boy.' Is there something you're trying to tell us?"

Helen grinned from ear to ear. "I got all this stuff at a garage sale yesterday, really cheap, so I didn't think you'd mind if it didn't match. Aren't these plastic pirate cups adorable?"

The ladies' eyes wandered from the wedding cake platter, to the Over-the-Hill dinner plates. Expressions of confusion were evident on their faces.

Ginger pushed her long red ponytail to one side, and in her most subdued social worker voice whispered, "Helen, are you feeling all right?"

Helen gazed at her friends, eyebrows raised. Noting their somber expressions, her demeanor abruptly flat lined. "What do you mean? I thought you would all remember and be so happy."

"Remember what?" asked Ginger, quietly eyeing the rest of the party goods.

Helen stared into the blank faces of her friends. "Today is our two-year anniversary … of meeting here … in Dante's. I thought a party would be so fun. Didn't any of you remember?"

Before they had a chance to respond, two hefty state troopers marched through the front door, scanning the area like sharks searching for prey. Their eyes locked on the five elderly women in the west corner.

"Helen!" boomed the lead trooper's deep, gravelly voice, "Front and center! Now!"

The men approached in long, serious strides. The women blanched. Estelle slipped behind Ruth and clutched her from behind.

Bella pushed to the front, shouting. "What do you want with our friend? You better not try to arrest her. My son-in-law is a big-time lawyer, you know! She's got rights. Whatever she did."

"I'm sure she didn't mean it," whimpered Estelle, poking her head out from behind Ruth.

"Not here to arrest anybody this time," the other man barked. Then they burst into laughter as each, in turn, leaned over and gave Helen a big hug.

The women's jaws dropped. Helen's skin flamed red from the base of her throat to the tip of her dark brown eyebrows.

"Everybody … I'd like to introduce Conrad and Trevor," she stuttered.

"Thank you for including us in your party this morning," said Trevor, who at 6'5" towered over the group. "But we can only stay a few minutes. We're still on duty."

"You can at least have a cup of coffee and a piece of cake," countered Helen. "I insist. Why don't you pull over another table next to ours."

"Yes, ma'am!" The men grinned.

Roger shook his head in amazement and turned to Desmond. "Okay, now the scene is complete! I'm going back into the kitchen."

"Whoa, whoa, whoa! Don't tell me those are the same state trooper dudes who came the day she crashed into the fire hydrant two years ago?"

"Yep. Unbelievable. Only Helen could pull that off." He rolled his eyes in disbelief.

Estelle lifted herself up on her tiptoes and whispered into Ruth's ear, "Are they going to arrest Helen?"

"No, dear, it doesn't seem so."

"Oh, good. Do you think I can still get my breakfast then? I would really like to have some scrambled eggs before I eat the cake. It's not good to have all those sweets on an empty stomach."

"Of course you can, dear. In fact, I think I will join you. I suddenly have a craving for a cheese omelet." Ruth pushed the cake to the side, grabbed a menu from the front counter, and sat down. The others soon followed suit.

The next half hour passed quickly. The diner filled to capacity as the women leisurely ate their breakfasts and the men polished off most of the cake. Several versions of Helen's misadventure with the fire hydrant were recalled, each with its own explicit, yet widely varying, details. An out of tune symphony of sounds surrounded the little group in the west corner, with all of their rowdy voices happily bouncing off the ivory walls. The time sailed smoothly by.

It was almost 10 o'clock when the first earsplitting shriek of automobile brakes cut through the normal restaurant clatter. The sound of shattering impacts followed...multiple crunching collisions with thunderous escalations. Conrad and Trevor sprang to their feet just as a blue SUV exploded through the west wall of Dante's Café just a few feet from where they were seated.

"OUT OF THE WAY! NOW!" the officers roared, wrenching the ladies from their chairs, and literally tossing them across the room as if they were rag dolls. They had barely cleared the space when the SUV flattened their tables before continuing on its hurling trajectory across the entire length of the dining room, finally plowing into the cashier's counter up front, where it came to a grinding halt. Seconds later, with one terrifying shudder, the entire west wall of the building crumbled and collapsed. Roger's antique cash register crashed to the ground, and all went silent.

Ruth lifted her head. She had been tossed out of the vehicle's path by Trevor, and had landed on her right hip before sliding along the tile floor. She now found herself wedged under another table further back in the room. She tried to move, but her head was swimming. Slowly, she came to a sitting position. Blood was pooling beneath her hand from a deep gash on her right forearm. "Is everyone okay?" she called in a tremulous voice.

"I'm here," Helen answered softly. "I think I'm okay. Ginger … Where are you?"

"Trapped under the Apocalypse tablecloth," came the muffled reply. "Get me out of here!"

Using a toppled chair for support, Helen slowly pulled herself off the floor and dusted the broken glass from her hair and face. "I'm coming!"

With Helen's help, Ginger managed to disentangle herself, and eventually stood on wobbly legs.

"Estelle and I are okay," called Bella from across the room. With Estelle's help, she pulled a jagged shard of glass from her ankle and applied pressure to the wound using a handful of baby-boy napkins. "We need to call 911, if anyone can find a phone."

"Already done," Conrad answered, quickly scanning the ladies to make sure they were okay.

Other faces began to emerge from beneath the rubble. Moans, groans, and cries could be heard from the many people who had been shaken and sprayed with debris.

"Help is on the way," Conrad announced. "Everyone, try to remain calm, and clear this area as soon as you can." Then he and Trevor ran toward the crumpled SUV. Together, they forcibly pried open the doors. They dragged a young couple from the front seats and pulled them to safety, just as smoke began pouring out of the engine.

Before anyone could stop her, Estelle pushed past her friends and jumped into the rear of the vehicle. "There are two babies back here," she screamed.

The smoke thickened. Roger vaulted over the remains of the antique cash register with a fire extinguisher, squirting white foam everywhere, while Estelle deftly unbuckled two car seats, passing one child to Bella and cradling the other close to her chest. Trevor jumped in and dragged her and the child to safety.

Helen and Ginger checked each other over and decided to tag team. Helen herded most of the guests into undamaged areas, gathered their belongings and generally tried to organize the chaos. Ginger followed up, writing down names and addresses on the back of the daily–special menu, while calming nerves with her strong but gentle social worker persona.

Desmond hauled some of the debris from the area, shoving remaining tables to the side, and sweeping broken glass away from the rest of the diners.

The first ambulance arrived within seven minutes. By then, Ruth, well into triage mode, had made a brief assessment of most of the injured patrons in the damaged area. She eagerly passed her notes and observations on to the EMTs and began searching for her friends.

Hordes of people: patrons, passersby, police, firefighters, and ambulance personnel streamed into Dante's Café, all trying to help. Ruth spotted Bella and Estelle huddled together in the midst of the mayhem, each still cradling a small child. She breathed a sigh of relief and pushed her way outside where over a dozen fire trucks and police cars jammed the streets. News helicopters hovered overhead, adding to the deafening noise. Her head throbbed.

She threaded her way through the crowd until she saw Ginger and Helen beside one of the emergency vehicles, handing over the information they had gathered to someone in uniform. Ruth joined them.

Conrad approached the ladies from behind, put his arms around the three women, and led them toward the ambulance. "Time for you superheroes to get checked out now," he said.

"We're okay," Ginger protested.

"I'm sure you are. But you're covered in glass, and you're probably going to be very sore from being thrown around."

Ruth stared into his eyes. "What about Estelle and Bella?" she asked.

"They're still inside. Trevor's rounding them up."

He looked down at the older women. After a brief hesitation, he added, "I'm sorry for tossing you around, but there was no other way to get you to safety on time. I hope you're all okay—no broken bones or anything."

Bella limped up to join her friends.

"You saved our lives. Who gives a damn about a few bumps and bruises? Or a broken leg," she added. "Hey, Doc," she called out to the nearest EMT, "you gotta look at my foot. It hurts."

"Where's Estelle?" asked Ruth, looking at Bella's bloody leg. "I thought you two were together."

"Yeah, well, we were, but I left her fighting with some lady cop back in there."

"About what?"

"You know Estelle," Bella shrugged, "she wouldn't hand

over the toddler she found. She kept saying that since she saved the kid's life, she had a right to keep him."

Conrad chuckled. "Don't worry, we'll get it all sorted. Now go get yourselves taken care of."

Helen looked down at her watch. "Wow. It's been nearly twenty-five minutes since the crash. It feels like a year."

"A long year," whispered Ruth. "And we all made it through."

Ginger began to tremble. "I'm cold," she said, fighting back a flood of tears. One of the EMTs placed a blanket over her shoulders and led the women away.

They waited together while the EMTs ruled out a fracture of Bella's foot, giving her a bandage and a prescription for pain medication instead of the cast she had insisted upon. They participated in the joint effort to convince Estelle to hand over the small child she'd been holding, to someone from Child Protective Services, after their barely conscious parents had been taken by ambulance to a local hospital.

Long after they were cleared to leave, the five of them remained, clinging to each other. They stood silently and watched as the wreckage of the SUV was pried from the restaurant and carted off on a flatbed truck. They listened as the sounds of panic gradually morphed into the drumbeat of hammers, installing large sheets of plywood to seal the open wound in Dante's west wing.

As more people arrived on the scene, the five old women

were gradually pushed farther back, until they were standing behind a police barrier across the street from the restaurant.

Another hour rolled by. Eventually, emergency vehicles fled to other emergencies. Crowds disbursed in search of more current excitement, and an uneasy quiet settled over the street.

Still, the ladies lingered, now huddled in Dante's parking lot.

"I've never been personally involved in anything like this before," whispered Ginger.

"It's not at all like what it looks like on television," added Estelle.

"Everything seems under control, so I suppose we should go home now." Ruth looked down at the rivulet design of dried blood on her beige sweater and slacks. She stroked the bandage someone had placed on her arm.

Bella broke into tears. "I don't want to go home yet. I keep thinking how close we came to dying back there … it made me realize how much I've come to depend on each of you batty old broads. You're my best buddies, and I just don't know how I'd manage without all of you." She mopped her tears with a clump of used tissues.

"Statistically speaking," Helen sniffed, putting her arm across Bella's shoulders, "this won't ever happen to us again. So, we're okay."

"Yes. By some miracle, none of us was seriously hurt, and we're all still together," said Ginger.

"Two miracles," Ruth added. "Trevor and Conrad. If not for

them …"

Estelle reached into the pocket of her floppy blue sweater for a tissue. Instead, her fingers curled around the small packet of birthday candles. She blinked back tears as she handed them to Helen, "I think these belong to you. And in case I forgot to say it, thank you very much for the party."

"But the party was ruined, and all the little gifts I got us were smashed," Helen sobbed.

"Yes." Ruth smiled. "But thank God, the best gifts are still alive and standing right here, still together."

"Look at it this way," added Bella with a sad, crooked smile. "None of us will ever forget this anniversary again… no matter how hard we try."

It took about another half hour, and another round of tears, before the five old ladies found the courage to climb into their individual cars. It was almost 2 pm before slowly, and reluctantly, they each began their long trek home.

CHAPTER 13—DANTE'S CLOSING

The ladies stood side by side, a silent amalgamation of bug-eyed women staring at the sign in the window. Bright red letters.

To all our valued customers:

Due to renovations

Dante's Café will be closed until further notice

"How could this be?" said Estelle, wringing her hands.

"I'm pretty sure Roger told us they expected to be open a day or two after the crash," said Helen.

"Yes, he did," Ruth agreed emphatically. "And I'm also sure he would have let us know if they intended to close completely. Something is very wrong."

The group pursed their lips and clenched their teeth.

Helen walked up to the window and brushed her hand across the dirty pane, smudging it further. She pushed her nose to the glass and tried to look in.

"What do you see?" asked Estelle. "Is Roger's body lying on the floor? Should we call the cops?"

Helen turned to look at her, a black splotch now imprinted on her nose. "You've been watching CSI again, haven't you?"

Estelle nodded. "They have a specialist who can tell a lot about the crime scene from blood splatter. Is there any blood on the walls…or on the ceiling?"

Ginger spit into a tissue, walked up to Helen, and tried to rub the black smudge off her friend's nose. That being done, she, Ruth, and Bella quickly shimmied up to the window and stared inside. Estelle edged closer but was too short to look over the sill. She tried taking little hops but couldn't get enough lift to give her a view of the interior.

"I don't see any blood," said Ginger. "But the place is a mess."

"No bodies on the floor," commented Bella.

"Well, what do you see?" Estelle continued hopping.

"A mop, a large dust bin, the tables all pushed to one side, and the wallpaper over the counter is half ripped down. The wall where the SUV crashed through is still roughly patched."

There was a loud scraping sound and the four ladies turned to find Estelle dragging a large metal bucket over to the window.

"What are you doing?" asked Ruth.

"I'm not leaving here until I see inside and know for certain that Roger is okay," Estelle said as she struggled to haul the bucket up to the window. Then she turned it upside down and tried to stand on top of it.

"Wait a minute, before you kill yourself!" yelled Ginger. "At least let me help you." She reached for Estelle's right hand.

"Okay. I'm almost up there now."

Estelle leaned on Ginger while placing her right foot on the bucket base. When she tipped backward, Ruth pushed her forward. Bella grabbed her left hand, and Helen helped place Estelle's left foot on the upside-down bucket.

"What the hell are you all doing?" boomed a deep voice from behind.

"We're trying to find Roger's body," said Estelle, turning briskly toward the man's voice and losing her balance again.

"Get down from there!" the man yelled.

In two steps he was between them, and before they could respond, he reached out with massive arms, lifted Estelle off the pail, and placed her on the ground near her friends. "Now stay there," he scolded, grabbing the bucket.

"But, Roger …"

"Roger's not here. No one's here, lady, just me."

"Is Dante's really closing?" asked Helen.

"They're already closed."

"But, for good?" Estelle asked, smoothing her rumpled coat.

The man shrugged.

"Who are you?" asked Ruth.

"Ernie."

"Are you the owner of Dante's?"

"No. Just a contractor."

"But Roger is still going to work here, right?" Helen asked, concern written in the deepening creases of her face.

"I have no idea, lady. I'm only here to do the renovations."

"But if it's being fixed up," said Ginger, "then it means they're not permanently shutting Dante's down, right?"

"I heard the place was sold," Ernie replied. "Happened over the weekend. Took everyone by surprise, I guess. No idea if it'll open again or not. Not my business." Bucket in hand, he turned and walked away, leaving the five forlorn ladies standing rigid and silent like soldiers at attention.

"What should we do now?" whispered Estelle. "I'm hungry."

They scanned the stores to the right and left.

"We could try the Coconut Bar and Grill a few doors down," said Helen.

"That's a smelly bar." Ruth shook her head, 'no'. "I don't want to go in there."

"Me neither," said Ginger, scratching a one-inch hive blooming at the base of her throat.

They turned around in a circle, searching the area, waiting for something to pop up on the horizon.

"There's a Chinese restaurant across the street," Ruth said at last. "The sign in the window says, 'American Breakfast Served'. I guess we could try that for today. I mean, as long as we're already here."

The group agreed. They left their cars in Dante's parking lot, walked to the intersection, and began their trek across the five-lane highway. Ruth, Helen, and Ginger were taller and quicker, and they easily ambled across the road. But Bella and Estelle were only halfway across when the light turned red. Cars edged forward and honked. Ruth and Ginger ran back into the intersection waving frantically, while Helen, shoulders at attention, blew her police department safety whistle. Eventually, Bella and Estelle made it across, and the ladies continued on to the Chinese restaurant without further incident.

"I dunno," said Bella, holding her water glass up to the light and staring at all the little bits of solid stuff floating inside. "This place is just not the same as Dante's."

The ladies had crowded around one wobbly Formica table in the middle of the restaurant. There were only two other customers in the place, sitting in an alcove near a small window.

Watercolor prints of Lotus blossoms hung crookedly on each wall, and the mingling aromas of burnt rice, grease, and orange-scented room freshener wafted through the air.

"I agree. It's twice as expensive, and the bagels taste funny," said Ruth.

"They taste Chinese," said Estelle. "Just like these eggs."

"How can hard-boiled eggs taste Chinese?" Helen asked. "And why are you trying to eat them with chop sticks?"

"Well, because we're here, and when in China, do as the Chinese do. Remember?"

"But we're not in China," interjected Ruth. "We're in Beaverton, so you can safely put the chop sticks down and eat with a fork."

"Okay." Estelle pouted.

"I really miss my hot poached eggs and bacon," lamented

Bella. "And don't tell me to be quiet and use my indoor voice! I'm upset. Cold, hard-boiled eggs and spare ribs with a Chinese bagel on the side is not my idea of an American breakfast." She sighed.

Ginger reached into her purse for a tube labeled 2% cortisone and began rubbing the cream onto her throat where a second hive had now blossomed. "So, what do you think we should do next week?"

"I have an idea. How about we meet at my house next week," offered Ruth. "It won't be anything fancy, but I certainly can have hot eggs and good bagels."

"And I hope we can have good coffee instead of this watery tea," said Bella.

"Absolutely. And in the meantime, let's see if we can find another breakfast place until Dante's opens again."

They all agreed.

Ruth reached for the bill that had been placed on their table by a thin Asian woman. "Ugh," she groaned. "We asked for separate checks when we came in, didn't we?"

"Absolutely," said Ginger, pulling the single piece of paper away from Ruth and staring at it." She began to laugh. "Here, Estelle, you take it and figure out what each of us owes."

Ginger handed the check to Estelle, who anxiously turned it upside down, sideways, and then right side up again.

Estelle fumbled in her purse. "I'm sorry, but I seem to have forgotten my reading glasses," she mumbled. "I think somebody else is going to have to decipher it."

Bella grabbed the paper from Estelle's hands and stared at it. Then she stared at Ginger with a mischievous grin." Choking down a giggle, she turned to Estelle. "It's okay, dear; Helen will take care of this one today." She tossed the bill to Helen.

"What am I supposed to do with the damn thing?" Helen squawked. "It's written in Chinese!"

"I'm sure you'll figure it out," said Ruth, grinning for the first time that day.

"Fine!" said Helen, "Today we divide. Seven bucks apiece, front and center now!"

"Wait a minute," said Estelle, pushing herself away from the table. "I've got to see if they sell lottery tickets here." She ambled up to the front counter and returned a few minutes later, lottery ticket in hand, and a big smile on her face.

"I don't know why you waste your money on those damn things," snorted Bella. "The chances of winning are none to impossible."

Estelle pouted. "But I did win once."

"Really? When?" asked Ginger.

"About a month ago." Estelle smiled. "I got one dollar and forty-nine cents."

"Forty-nine cents?" Ruth questioned. "I thought all lottery tickets only came in single dollar amounts."

"Well, yes," Estelle reflected, "but the day I won the dollar, I also found forty-nine cents on the sidewalk near my car, so I counted that as part of my winnings,"

"I rest my case," said Bella as the ladies each placed their cash on the table. Helen counted it and sorted the bills into increasing denominations, making sure they were all facing the same direction. She secured the cash to the center of the table with a bottle of soy sauce. Then she looked up at her friends, and her smile disappeared.

"Listen," said Helen, "before we go, I have something I want to share." She hesitated.

"Sounds serious," said Ruth.

"Yes. It could be."

"Okay. Spill it," grumbled Bella.

"I originally wasn't going to bring this up, but..."

"Just spit it out," said Bella.

Helen took a deep breath. "Bill went to see the doctor again last week because of that lingering cough he's had."

"He's still coughing?" asked Ruth. "It's been a long time."

"I know," Helen replied. "He just hasn't been able to shake it. Antibiotics haven't worked, so they sent him for X-rays, and the doctor called last night." Helen bit her lip.

"Doctors calling your home at night is not a good thing," said Bella, shaking her head.

"It seems the radiologist saw a shadow on Bill's right lung." Helen continued. "He goes for a biopsy on Friday. That's it. I just wanted you all to know. Please keep your fingers crossed for us, okay?"

Ruth reached out first. "You always have to check these things out, but most of the time they turn out to be nothing," she said. "I'm sure he'll be okay, but call me if you need anything at all, okay?"

"Do you want me to go with you and Bill on Friday?" Ginger asked.

"No. We'll be okay. But thank you for asking." Helen brushed away a stray tear. "It's so scary. We've been married for forty-two years. He's such a pain in the ass, but I can't imagine my life without him."

"Then don't," said Estelle. "He's with you now, and God willing, he will be with you for another forty-two years. Just keep positive thoughts and let us know how we can help."

The ladies ended up staying at the Chinese American restaurant for another half hour, ordering two more pots of jasmine tea, and chipping in another two bucks each toward the bill.

CHAPTER 14—ESTELLE'S PHONE CALLS

Estelle settled comfortably in her living room recliner and reached for the telephone. It was exactly 4:00 p.m. Tuesday afternoon when she began to dial.

Call #1

The phone rang three times before Ruth answered. "Hello…"

"Hi, Ruthie. It's me."

"Estelle?"

"Yes. Listen, I'm not really good at finding my way around new places. I was wondering if I could carpool with you tomorrow when we go for breakfast."

"Estelle, we're meeting here at my house tomorrow, remember? So I'm not driving."

"Oh, that's right. It wouldn't work then. Okay. Never mind."

Click.

4:03 p.m. Call #2

"This is the residence of Helen and Bill Kahn. There is no one home at this moment. If you'd like to leave a message …"

Click.

4:05 p.m. Call #3

After dialing, Estelle stood up and walked to the broad windowsill in her living room. With the receiver tucked between her shoulder and ear, she started plucking dead leaves off the small geranium plant she had purchased the previous week. She was so engrossed in trying to make the leaf pattern symmetrical that she was startled by the man's voice answering her call.

"Who is this?" she challenged.

"You made the call, lady. Who are you looking for?"

Estelle took the receiver away from her ear and stared at the phone for a moment.

"I don't remember," she said, and hung up.

Click.

4:08 p.m. Call #4

The phone was picked up on the first ring by the same man as before.

"Hello."

"Aldon? Is that you?"

"Yes. Who is this?" he asked.

"It's Bella."

"Bella?"

"No, I mean it's Estelle. I'm looking for Bella."

"Oh. Hi Estelle. Hold on a minute, I'll get her."

"Bella!!! Telephone!!!"

"Who is it?"

"It's Estelle looking for Bella. I mean, Estelle is looking for you. Oh God, that batty lady's even got me confused now."

"Shh … she'll hear you."

"I doubt it," Aldon muttered.

"Hi, Estelle, what can I do for you?"

"We're supposed to be going to Ruth's house for our breakfast tomorrow morning, right?" She continued absentmindedly plucking the geranium leaves.

"Yes. That's the way we left it last week. Why? Did you hear anything different?"

"No. It's just that I don't like driving alone to new places. I'm always afraid of getting lost. So I was wondering if we could carpool, and I could come with you."

"You know, that would be nice," Bella replied. "I also get nervous about getting lost, so maybe between the two of us, we can find our way. I'll print out the directions and drive, and you can be the navigator and tell me when to turn. How does that sound?"

"Great! I really appreciate it. I'll practice tonight: *right turn, left turn, right turn, left turn!* How does that sound?"

"You don't have to work so hard, Estelle, I gave up making left turns four years ago after my last car accident. I only make right turns now. I'll pick you up at 8:30 tomorrow morning."

Estelle smiled gently, placing her little plant back on the window ledge, its two remaining leaves nicely balanced, one on either side.

CHAPTER 15—THE CARPOOL

It was 8:40 when Bella pulled up in front of Estelle's house and honked the horn. Estelle stuck her head outside, waved to her friend, and ducked back in to grab her coat. Seconds later, coat in hand, she ambled toward the car.

"Sorry I'm late," Bella said as Estelle struggled to buckle her seat belt. "There was a bit more traffic than I figured."

"That's okay. I'm excited to see where Ruth lives, although I feel funny going without bringing something."

"Well, I brought an apple pie, so we can say it's from both of us. But since we are already late, I will need a navigator more than ever. Here, let me show you the directions." Bella unfolded two pages of a computer printout and leaned close to Estelle.

"Okay, this first page is just a map, starting with where I live and ending at Ruth's house. Ruth lives on SW Briarwood Place. This dark line is the route we need to take."

Estelle removed her glasses, cleaned the lenses on the bottom of her sweater, and pushed them back onto the bridge of her nose.

Bella then turned to the second page. "These are the written directions."

"Boy, this looks complicated," said Estelle. "What are all those numbers?"

"That's how Google writes directions. Haven't you ever seen Google directions before?"

"Well, I've heard about Google, but I've never met him this close up before."

Bella rolled her eyes. "I know how to get to TV Highway." Bella turned back to the map page and pointed to the dark-blue line. Then she turned to the directions page. "See here where it says '*Turn right onto TV Highway?*'"

Estelle nodded.

"That's the same place I just showed you on the map."

Estelle nodded again.

"Over here in this column it says we have to stay on TV Highway for 1.5 miles. And in the little print on the next line, it says how many minutes it should take and the total mileage of how far we've come. Pretty simple, huh?"

Estelle took off her glasses again, dropped them on her lap, brought the direction page up close to her nose, and squinted.

"Bella?"

"Yes?"

"I can't read the little print."

"That's okay, honey." Bella sighed.

"Can you read the big print, like where it says, '*Follow the signs to Murray Boulevard?'"*

"Yes, I can see that. And after that, we have to turn right. Right?"

"Yep. You got it. Let's go. It's already 8:45, and we've got to hurry in order to make it there by 9:00."

"And don't forget we still have to stop at the little grocery store up the road," said Estelle as they pulled away from the curb.

"What for?"

"I want to get some flowers. You know, I feel funny going without bringing something," Estelle repeated. "I could run in real quick and get a nice bunch of daffodils."

"But ..."

"Turn right, NOW!" Estelle screeched.

Bella clenched her teeth and made a sharp right turn into the narrow drive of a local convenience store.

"See, I've been practicing giving directions!"

"Very good, dear," growled Bella.

Estelle hopped out of the car as soon as it stopped rolling and ran into the little grocery. "I'll be right back ..." she shouted over her shoulder. It was another ten minutes before she returned, clutching two bunches of daffodils and a lottery ticket. "Okay, let's go," she chirped happily.

Bella stopped biting her nails and gunned the engine, leaving a patch of rubber on the asphalt driveway as she made a right turn onto TV Highway. They reached Murray Boulevard ten minutes later and turned right. The miles flew by as the two ladies chatted about ceiling leaks, the length of dog tails, and the pursuit of a homemade chocolate chip cannoli. Eventually, Bella looked at the road signs and asked Estelle to check the map. "Do you know where we are?"

"No. Don't you?"

"You're the navigator, Estelle! You're supposed to be keeping track of these things. I forgot the name of the road we're supposed to turn on. What do the directions say?"

Estelle fumbled with the two pages. "This one says TV Highway."

"We passed that already, Estelle. We're on Murray. How far are we supposed to go?"

Estelle took off her glasses and held the directions page up to her nose. "There's one that says seven-dot-four, and another that says three-dot-six, and another that says eleven-dot-three. Which one do you want?"

Bella felt her face turn red. "I hate getting lost even more than I hate being late. Can't you read the directions? Where do we go next after Murray Boulevard?"

Estelle kept switching from the map page to the direction page.

Bella bit down on her lower lip and tried to calm her breathing as she felt herself slipping into panic mode. "Forget the map. Just look at the directions sheet. Do you see where it says TV Highway?"

"Yes." Estelle nodded.

"Good. Now right under that, it says turn right at Murray Boulevard."

"Yes, I see that."

"Good. You're doing fine. What is the next line under that?"

"It says Turn left onto SW Scholls Ferry Road."

"Scholls Ferry ... Estelle, we passed that already! Why didn't you tell me?"

Estelle scratched her nose and looked up timidly. "Because it said turn left, and last night you told me that you didn't make left turns anymore, so I was waiting for the next right turn."

"Dear God, please help me..." Bella muttered, swerving across three lanes of traffic to get off at the next rapidly approaching intersection. She hooked a sharp left onto SW Barrows and then made a quick right into the parking lot of a Great Clips Salon.

Estelle looked concerned. "Are you okay? You look all flustered. I can drive if you like. You'd probably be a better navigator than me anyhow."

Bella stared at her friend and grimaced. "I'm fine, dear," she said gently through clenched teeth. "Can I please see the map? I've got to plot us another route." She took the map and studied it for several minutes. "We can still get to Ruth's this way," she said, pointing to the map page again, "although, it may take a little longer. Now try to remember this, dear, if you can. In a few miles, we are going to turn right onto SW Scholls, then right onto SW 135th, then right onto SW Hawks Beard. Got it?"

"I think so. Do you think they will wait for us for breakfast? It's past 9:30 already and I'm hungry."

"I'm sure Ruth will have plenty of food. Let's try this again," Bella said as she guided the car onto the main road.

"Right onto SW Scholls, right onto SW 135th, right onto SW Hawks Beard," Estelle kept repeating as they whisked along.

"So far, so good," said Bella when they turned onto Hawks Beard. She guided the car over to the side of the road by a small farm stand and put it in park. "Okay, we should be pretty close by now, but getting around in her development and finding Briarwood is the tricky part. Can I see the map again, Estelle?"

Estelle looked up, panic in her eyes. "I didn't know we still needed it."

"Of course we do. We're not there yet. And we'll also need it to find our way home again. Where is it, honey?"

"Well, the daffodils started leaking, so I wrapped the paper around the stems to keep my dress from getting wet."

The soggy paper dissolved into several pieces as Estelle peeled it from the flower stems in an effort to hand it to her friend.

"Oh, Estelle!"

"What are we going to do now?" Estelle whimpered.

Bella took a deep breath. "We call Ruth and find out where we are supposed to go from here. That's what we do."

Ruth picked up the telephone on the second ring. "Bella? Is that you?"

"Yes."

"Is Estelle with you?"

"Yessirree."

"It's 10:15, and we were really getting worried."

"I'm sorry. We got lost."

"Have you any idea where you are?"

"Somewhere near your development, I think. I pulled over by a little farm stand called Rudy's. It's on SW Hawks Beard Street."

"I know exactly where that is, and you're only a few minutes away. I'm sending Gordon out to get you. Hang tight…he'll be there in a second, driving a blue Camaro."

"Fantastic!"

Bella turned off the ignition. A wave of relief washed over her as she leaned back into the seat. "Thank you, God," she whispered.

Estelle looked down at her hands and examined the daffodils carefully. They were beginning to droop. "I hope Gordon gets here soon," she whispered mournfully. "I think these flowers need more water. And I really do have to pee."

CHAPTER 16 — SEX TALK AND WAITERS

The next Wednesday morning was cold, clear, and bright. Sunshine after two weeks of rain. The ladies were seated in a small booth at Shari's restaurant, located only a mile from Helen's house. The only vacant booth they could find was wedged between the game room and the kitchen. Estelle was busily stuffing small bits of tissue in her ears to blot out the dual sounds of the arcade machines and the clatter of dishes.

"God, I miss having sex," Ginger blurted, combing her mahogany-red hair with long manicured nails.

"What?" asked Estelle.

"I said, I miss having sex. I spent thirty years as a social worker in a senior residence, but I don't think the discussion of sex came up more than a handful of times. I wonder now if it was anything I said, or didn't say, that closed the door on those conversations."

The ladies glanced at each other knowingly.

"They do fizzle out in the later years, don't they?" Bella sighed. "Aldon just turned seventy-eight, but he hasn't been good in that department for at least a decade. Not something you can talk about with most people."

"Well, Howard is only seventy-five. It was the diabetes that did him in, I'm sure of it," said Ginger, putting three heaping teaspoons of sugar in her coffee and stirring vigorously. She paused while the waitress refilled the breadbasket. "He was such a passionate lover when we met. I still remember how he used to pin me up against the wall." A bright smile splashed across her face. "He was so sure of himself, even our first time in the deserted banquet room of the Marriot, in China. I never imagined it would end so soon."

Two young waiters inched closer to the group of old ladies. One began refilling the coffee cups; the other leaned over Ginger's shoulder and began topping off her water glass.

"What I remember most are all the showers Bill and I would take together." Helen's eyes half-closed and her lips curled in a quiet grin. "He'd wash me down, then lift me up. Those were the days, when I was slimmer, and he was stronger. I think the contours of our bodies were permanently imprinted in the steamed walls of our first little apartment."

"Just a few years ago, right?" Ruth laughed.

"Yeah. Just a few."

"What happened a few years ago?" asked Estelle.

"Was that before or after you married him?" Ginger asked.

"Both," Helen answered. "We had stamina in those days. Not that you'd know it from looking at us now." She pursed her lips in a half smile and started pulling tiny fuzz balls off her purple slacks.

"So," Bella asked, "was Bill your first?"

"Oh yeah. First and only," Helen replied. "In those days you were expected to be a virgin when you married. Or, if you could keep a secret, maybe you'd be with him before the wedding. But that ring had better be permanently clamped onto your finger before you messed around."

Two more servers hovered, clearing dishes and bringing small baskets of freshly baked muffins. Estelle turned and looked into the eyes of the young waitress directly behind her. The girl had green hair with blue and orange streaks, a ring through her left nostril, and another through her right eyebrow. She caught Estelle's glance, dropped five paper napkins on the table, and walked off.

"I don't think we ever got such good service at Dante's," Bella stated. "I think we should talk about sex more often."

"What?" Estelle strained forward.

"Oh, for God's sake, Estelle! Pull those plugs out of your ears!"

"Huh?"

Ruth reached over and yanked a wad of paper from Estelle's right ear. "We're talking about sex, that's what," she said dropping the crumpled tissue onto the floor.

Estelle pulled the tissue out of her left ear.

"Well, why didn't you say so? I was trying to block out the sound of the arcade games. Is Josie coming today?"

"No, dear," said Ginger. "She's in California this week

visiting her grandkids."

"Changing the subject a bit, I miss Dante's," said Bella. "I mean this place is okay, much better than that Chinese restaurant, but it's awfully far from where I live, and I just don't want to add another fifteen minutes onto my trip. Maybe we should continue rotating houses until we find a place that suits us all."

Ruth picked up the straw near her water glass, tore the tip of the covering paper off, and blew into the plastic tube, sending the empty paper sleeve flying across the table. It landed on Ginger's chest, slid underneath her low-cut yellow blouse, and got wedged between her breasts.

Ginger grabbed the paper sleeve, dunked it in her water glass, and threw the wet glob back at Ruth.

"Well, I hosted last time," said Ruth, tossing the wet paper back at Ginger.

"Will you two cut it out!" yelled Bella, tearing a breakfast roll in half and throwing pieces at both of them. "I'll volunteer to host breakfast next week if we can't find any other place before then."

"And hopefully you won't get lost driving to your own place like you did coming to mine." Ruth smiled sarcastically.

Bella picked up the glop of wet paper in front of Ginger and threw it at Ruth, rolling her eyes toward Estelle.

"Okay, it's official … Bella's place next week," said Helen. "And just so you know, if I end up driving Estelle, you are not getting any daffodils!"

Ruth turned to Ginger, who was staring, dreamily, into space.

"Earth to Ginger! Earth to Ginger! Where are you?" she sang.

Ginger looked up and blushed. "I'm in the Breakers Hotel on the boardwalk of Atlantic City, in the summer of 1959."

"And ..."

"And I'm soaking in an oversized porcelain bathtub filled with hot salty sea water, and a six-foot hunk named Jake."

"Jake? Who's Jake?" they all screamed.

Ginger giggled. "Not gonna tell you!"

"You have to," Helen insisted. "It's written in our by-laws!"

Estelle nudged closer to Ruth. "Do we have by-laws?"

"No, dear. Helen was just joking."

"I want dates, times, and all the details," insisted Helen. "Now!"

"Well," said Ginger, shooing away two more waitresses, "most of you ladies were only married once, whereas Ruth and I had several false starts. I mean, even if you were a virgin the first time around, not that I necessarily was, but still, that certainly wasn't the case by the time you hooked up with number two. Or three. Or whatever."

"So which one was Jake, number two or three or whatever?" Bella asked between a round of hiccups.

Ginger giggled again. "Actually, he was my second lover, but my first husband. And that's all I am going to say. Aside from the fact that he was drop-dead gorgeous, Italian, and my parents almost disowned me when they found out we'd eloped."

"Well, he certainly sounds delightfully yummy. So, why'd

you two break up?"

"Let's see, how I can put this delicately … after a while, he found monogamous relationships boring. I was young, and might have been able to overlook some of his indiscretions, but when he insisted on a ménage à trois, I drew the line."

"Oh," said Bella, raising her eyebrows. "Now this is getting interesting." She looked up and saw a new group of waitresses hovering. As soon as she made eye contact, they melted away.

"Don't even ask for any more details, cause that's all you're gonna get." Ginger pushed her plate way and started applying her new pink lipstick.

"Okay, so when did you meet husband number two?" Helen asked.

"You can actually blame my parents for that mistake. They were so relieved when I divorced Jake that they bought me a consolation gift: an all-expense ticket on a very exclusive two-week singles cruise to Costa Rica. Supposed to be only for high-class, well-bred folks. They even had a matchmaker on board, for an extra fee, of course. Very expensive, but they paid for it all. That's where I met Henry."

"So, was he high-class, and rich?" asked Bella, dredging her roll through maple syrup.

"Nope. He was our waiter."

"You went on an exclusive trip and came home with the waiter?"

"Yeah." Ginger smiled, blotting her lipstick on a cloth

napkin. "It's strange, the things you learn about yourself in foreign situations. Turns out, I didn't really like the high-class rich guys. They were mostly fakes, living off the wealth of their parents. All they wanted was to get laid, to put another notch in their belt and move on. But Henry, well, he was sweet. He was from Argentina and was working his way into a better life."

"And your parents let you marry him?" asked Ruth.

"They had no choice. We were married on board, by the captain. He was already my husband by the time we got back to the States." She continued smiling.

"Oh, my God," said Helen. "You did that to your poor parents twice?" She waved away another waiter. "So, how long did that one last?"

"About two weeks. Unbeknownst to me, my folks hired a private detective to do a background check on him. That's when we found out that he already had at least one other wife in Argentina. Ah, poor Henry. He looked so sad when we finally had to say goodbye."

"So when did you finally meet Howard?" Ruth dismissed the waitress who was trying to fill her coffee cup for the fifth time.

"That was two years later. I was twenty-five by then, and he was thirty-one. We met in Shandong Province, China, during a monsoon. I was on vacation, staying at the Marriot, and he was there during the start-up phase of his import/export business. It was love at first sight. When I called home and told my folks that I had just met the man of my dreams, mom started to cry. Who could have imagined that I had to go all the way to China to meet a nice Jewish guy?"

Bella's cell phone rang. "What? What!" Her face blanched. "When? Okay. I'll be right there!" She turned to her friends. "Bonnie just went into labor. She's nearly a month early! I've got to get to the hospital!"

"Breathe, Bella, breathe! Do you want one of us to drive you?"

"No, but thanks for offering. I'll call you tonight. I've gotta go." Bella scooped up her purse and ran out of the door, screaming. "Someone please pick up my check and I'll pay you back later!"

"I got it!" Ruth shouted.

"Let us know how she is…" Helen yelled after her.

The ladies shared a collective sigh.

"Never a dull moment," Ruth muttered. "Listen, I've got to get going as well. It's almost 11:00, and I've got to babysit for the grandkids today." She stood and reached for her sweater. "As soon as anyone hears from Bella, pass it along, okay?" Then she turned and pointed a finger at Ginger. "This conversation is to be continued at Bella's next week, God willing. Got it?"

"Yeah, but don't be in such a rush for my story because next week it will be your turn to tell all!"

"Yeah … well, we'll see about that." Ruth grinned broadly as she slid out the door.

CHAPTER 17—ESTELLE'S EMAIL

Hi enveryonwwwwww. This is my ist email, so ii iope   ucun red it. I just wanted to tell you that I mewt Helen in Costco last night and she said to tell you all that Bill's biopsy just came back. H e has some weid type of lung infedction, but no cancer. She wanted to tell you all, bvu t her computer broke,I o I sid I would truy to sendt a emal to you all and share the good news. SSSSSsssje is going Ot meet us neXGT WWEDNESDY AT BELLAS HOUSE. SEEE YOU ALL THEn. esTELLe.

pS Bojo has aaaarived nd he and bonnie are doing great.!

CHAPTER 18—RUTH'S JOURNAL #2

Gordon searched from one room to the next. Where was she? He drew the paneled curtains aside and stared into the small yard. Lots of flowers. The lawn needed mowing again.

"Ruth!" he called out. No response. He wandered down the hall, straightening a row of slightly tilted paintings as he went. The door to the guest bedroom was ajar. He pushed it open and saw her hunched over her laptop. Not wanting to be intrusive, he padded quietly on the thick carpet until he stood directly behind her chair. She was typing and crying. He placed his wide hands on her shoulders and looked down.

Startled, Ruth screamed, simultaneously pulling away from his touch and slamming down the top of her computer. "What are you doing?" She swiveled around and stared at him with seething eyes.

"Whoa … what did I do wrong this time?" he asked, hands lifted in surrender.

"You know I don't like you reading over my shoulder. This is private. You have no right to read it unless I tell you!"

"Honey, I didn't read a word of it," he lied. "Honest. Just the title. Why are you so upset?"

"None of your business," she snapped. "You wouldn't understand, anyway."

"Ruthie ..."

"What?"

"Tell me what's wrong."

"No." Ruth pulled a tissue from her pocket and wiped her eyes.

"Ruthie, don't be like that. I love you. Tell me." He placed his hands on her shoulders again. This time she didn't shrug them off. '*Progress*', he thought.

"I'm just writing in my journal. That's all. It's private."

"I thought your writing class disbanded a couple of weeks ago."

"It did," she said, grabbing at a nearby tissue box. "But I decided that I like writing. It makes me feel good."

Gordon tilted his head and looked at her with an incredulous expression. "This is feeling good?"

"Well, maybe not today."

"So what's bothering you, honey?"

"I just feel alone. And unloved."

"Ruthie, we've been through this a thousand times. You are surrounded by people who love you. And you've always got me, you know."

"Yeah, I know."

"And tons of friends."

"Yeah."

"And your breakfast buddies."

She nodded.

"And the kids."

Silence.

"Is this about the kids again?"

She nodded. Another tear escaped.

"Can I see what you wrote?"

Reluctantly, she agreed. "But only this one time, because you asked nicely," she whispered, opening the laptop and moving away.

Gordon kissed the top of her head and began to read.

Ruth's Private Journal

It's all about circles you see. Family that is. We live in circles. Years ago Gordon and I made a circle. I can still visualize it, holding hands under the chupah, vowing to be with each other forever ... no matter what. And then the children started coming; David, Annise, and Lillian. And our circle grew. This was our world. Often not knowing what the next day would bring, trying to make prudent decisions, forging ahead as a family, getting by as best we could. We clung tightly to each other in those days; one unit, one circle. Until they grew up and went away. The kids that is. Gordon and I stayed together pretending we were still a family. But our circle now had dents, missing sections and broken links.

Memories of my own childhood are skewed. I can't recall a

circle from my youth. I don't remember anyone cheering me on, encouraging. Determined not to repeat the past, did I cling to my own babies too tightly?

All in retrospect of course: How proud when each was toilet trained, beaming at kindergarten scribbles, burning telephone wires when they were chosen ... for anything. I rooted for them at soccer, gymnastics, tennis, karate, dance, football, and the endless array of school orchestra and chorus performances. I gladly coughed up the cash for prom night tuxedos and corsages.

Then came sleep away camps, first jobs, college applications... What are they doing so far from home? For six months after they left I didn't change the sheets so I could keep their scent, never quite admitting they had gone.

I am unsure of the defining lines of my circle these days. The children's beds empty, Gordon remains by my side. Blessing, some days. Tiresome others. Bent, bruised, but still here.

My youngest called last Tuesday. Her sister called three hours later. Tears, fears, problems. You always make me feel better mom. Just wanted you to know. Thank you. Love you. Gotta go. Funny how they, being made of such independent stuff, still call when they are upset or sick. Not that they ever listen or take my advice. Occasionally they share a triumph. For me it is a quick fix, 30 seconds to hear the sound of their voice. Perhaps 30 minutes if they are stuck in traffic. Then they are off again. Do they understand the sound of their voice, however brief, completes my circle? Probably not.

A text message after a hard week stated she was okay but didn't want to talk. She needed time with her family ... to heal, to mend. Her family. I was not included. I am not in her circle, though she will forever be in mine. It is a hard lesson to learn.

Ruth had moved to the rocking chair in the corner by the window; her hands clasped in her lap. Gordon finished reading, walked over and pulled her up. He wrapped his arms around her and held her as she cried into his shoulder.

"You were, and still are, the best mother in the world."

"Do you really think so?"

"Yes. And so do the kids."

"But they grew up and left."

"Yes. Isn't it wonderful?"

She looked up at him and sniffled. "Do you really think so?"

"Of course. Would you rather they be still lying around our house like Edith's kids, unable to find a job or a spouse?"

She shook her head no.

"How about Sandra and Marv's kids, one locked up and the other on drugs?"

"No. Of course not."

"Our kids are strong, happy, and independent. And it is all because of you."

"Us," she added.

"We were good parents. But still, it was mostly you, and that is something to be very proud of."

"But they don't need me anymore," she whimpered.

The phone rang. Gordon picked up the receiver.

"Hello … Hi honey … what? Hold on a minute, she's right here."

Gordon turned and looked at his wife. "It's Lillian, for the fourth time today. She's got herself into some kind of pickle again and needs your help," he said with raised eyebrows and a sort of half smile as he handed over the phone. He could just about hear the first words of his youngest daughter before Ruth put the phone to her ear.

"Mom, I really could use your advice on this … I just don't know what to do …"

Ruth wiped the last tear away with the back of her hand and sat back down in the rocking chair. "Of course I have a minute, dear. Tell me what's wrong."

Gordon looked at her. She was back: strong, confident, in full mother mode. He took a deep breath and left the room, knowing that for the moment, her circle was complete.

CHAPTER 19—ESTELLE AND DAVID

David's hands were shaking as he steered the 1996 blue Chevy into the hotel's circular driveway. He mopped his forehead with a plaid handkerchief and stuffed it back in his shirt pocket. "See. No problem getting here. I told you so."

Estelle kept her mouth shut. The ninety-minute trip from Beaverton to Cannon Beach had taken three hours. The line of cars behind them now extended over the horizon.

Estelle looked around. She could see the water and the top of Haystack Rock. "I can't believe we're really doing this."

"Why not? Everyone else goes on vacation. Getting away for a long weekend is just what we needed. I just hope you packed everything this time. Did you remember my pajamas?"

"Yes, dear."

"And my tan slacks?"

"Yes."

"And all our medications?"

"Yes, I've got it all. Now stop bothering me!"

A young man in uniform greeted them. "Valet parking?"

David nodded, handing off a five-dollar bill as he hauled

himself out of the car.

Their luggage, consisting of one large suitcase and one small travel bag, was placed on a luggage cart by a hotel porter. David parted with another five dollars when the man escorted them to their seventh-floor suite and placed the luggage on top of the king-size bed. When he left, David and Estelle stared around at their luxurious new surroundings.

"Wow," whispered Estelle. "This is a really beautiful room. Are you sure we can afford it?"

"For our fifty-second anniversary? Why not!" He smiled broadly, puffing out his chest with great pride. He glanced in the mirror and slicked back the thinning circle of white hair that fringed his head. "I am now going to be indisposed for a few minutes," he announced as he picked up a complimentary newspaper from the nightstand and headed toward the bathroom. "Why don't you start unpacking? And I really do hope you didn't forget anything this time," he repeated as he disappeared behind the door.

Estelle drew back the curtains and walked onto a large balcony overlooking the ocean. The sun was shining, the air smelled sweet. It was wonderful. After a few minutes, she went inside again, inspecting the refrigerator, the coffee maker, and the television. All in working order. Nothing would spoil this weekend. It was perfect. Then she opened the lid of her suitcase and out jumped the cat.

"Oh God!" Her hands flew across her mouth to stifle the

scream that had already escaped.

"Something wrong?" David's coarse voice careened through the closed door.

"No, dear," she squeaked.

"Sounds to me like you forgot something important."

"No, in fact, we may even have a bit more than we need." Estelle bit her lip.

"If you say so. I'll be awhile. You okay to keep unpacking?"

"Take your time, dear. I'll manage."

Estelle looked around the room for the huge gray animal. "Daisy? Daisy! Here girl," she whispered. But the cat was gone.

"He's going to kill me," she mumbled to herself. "That's it. It's all over. I'm dead. Dead on my fifty-second wedding anniversary."

"Meow."

Estelle spun around. Daisy had bolted out to the balcony, jumped up on the narrow handrail, and was staring down at the beach, seven stories below, where a flock of seagulls had just landed.

"Oh God ..." Estelle whimpered.

She tiptoed onto the balcony, slowly extending her hands toward the back end of the cat, but before she was able to grab her, Daisy leaped onto the outdoor lounge and bounded into the room again. Estelle checked the cushion where Daisy had landed. There was only one pulled thread. Maybe no one would notice if she flipped the cushion over. Thank goodness it was reversible.

"Daisy," Estelle whispered. No cat. She looked in the closet. No cat. She looked under the desk in the small alcove that entitled the hotel to call this room a suite. No cat. Finally, she lowered herself to the floor and bent forward to search under the bed.

David walked out of the bathroom to find his wife on the floor, bum up waving at him.

"What the heck are you doing, Estelle? Did you fall?"

Estelle pulled her head out from under the bed, made a half turn, and flopped into a sitting position. "Um, no. I–I was just looking for ... an earring."

"Well, you have two of them on. How many were you wearing?"

Estelle reached for her ears. "Oh, silly me," she said. "I thought I had dropped it."

"I think you're losing it, Estelle. I mean, you're only seventy-eight. I'm eighty-two, and my brain is supposed to turn to mush before yours, but I think you're winning the race, dear. Can I help you up?"

She nodded.

David reached down and helped Estelle to her feet.

"This is supposed to be our luxurious getaway weekend. Breakfast in bed, room service, maid service, fancy stuff. You're not supposed to lift a finger. Just what you wanted, I thought. Instead you look sick as a dog. Are you coming down with something?"

Estelle sat on the edge of the bed, her face flushed. David put his hand on her forehead, checking for fever.

"I think some fresh air will do you good. Forget the unpacking." He stared at the suitcase, still brimming with clothes. "Just come on down to the beach with me, and we'll take a little stroll along the water's edge. Kinda like we did in the old days." His eyes were smiling.

"I can't, David. Not now."

David's smile turned to a frown. "Why not?"

"I-I'm just not feeling right. I think I would like to lie down for a few minutes. I'm sure it will pass. Why don't you go without me? For about an hour or so. I'm sure I'll feel better by then."

David sighed deeply; his shoulders drooped. "Okay, but this is a hell of a way to start a second honeymoon. I really thought we'd get off to a better start this time."

As soon as David left the room, Estelle ran into the bathroom and splashed cold water on her face. "Now think, old girl, just think. What to do." She took a deep breath and lifted her chin. "First thing …" She spoke out loud. "Find the cat." It turned out that Daisy was curled up on a goose down pillow on the top shelf of the closet. With the pointy end of a wooden hanger, Estelle tried to poke the beast, but Daisy only moved farther back on the shelf and resumed her nap.

"Okay, Plan B," she muttered. "Got to provide for the stupid animal." She reached for the telephone and called the front desk.

"Front desk, may I help you?"

"Yes. This is … Miss Smith … in room 205. I have a hypothetical question. By any chance are pets allowed in this hotel?"

"Absolutely not, ma'am. Under no circumstances are any animals allowed in this facility. In fact, we advertise as a hypoallergenic environment. Unless, of course, it is a service dog, in which case only specific rooms are designated."

"Have you ever booked any service cats?"

"Not so far."

"Hum. Okay." She hung up.

Estelle exchanged her leather shoes for sandals, buckled them tightly, put the *Do Not Disturb* sign on the door, and made a beeline for the gift shop on the main level. She went directly to the woman behind the counter.

"I was wondering if you could help me, please. My husband and I have just purchased a few beautiful plants from the florist, and I was hoping to find a box to put them in. You know, something you might be discarding. We could put the plants in the box, and I wouldn't be afraid of watering them, in case they leaked, you know, so it wouldn't spoil the carpet."

The saleswoman smiled pleasantly and disappeared into the back of the store. She returned carrying an empty twelve-by-fifteen-inch cardboard box labeled *Perfecto Condoms.* "Will this do?"

"Perfecto!" Estelle beamed.

"Anything else I can help you with?"

"Yes. I'll take two packages of the dried tuna fish, and two of these small decorative bowls, and several plastic bags, please."

The saleswoman never batted an eye. She handed all the supplies to Estelle, who paid in cash, and scrambled back up to her room, loot in hand.

Estelle checked her watch. There was only a half hour left until David was due to return. She would have to move fast. She cleared a space on the floor of the closet and shoved the box in the corner. She grabbed a bunch of paper towels from the bathroom, spread several layers of them down beside the box, and placed the decorative bowls on top. Then she opened one packet of tuna fish, which she dumped into the first bowl covering the $10.99 sticker, and filled the matching bowl with water.

"Kitty litter ... and we're done. Come on, old girl, you can do this," she whispered. She checked on Daisy, who had rolled onto her back and was sleeping spread-eagle on the goose down pillow, snoring lightly. Grabbing the plastic bags, she left the room again, this time finding her way down to the beach. The sun was very bright. She had forgotten both her sunscreen and her hat. Perspiration rolled down her face.

By the time Estelle found an isolated area, she was exhausted. She sat down in the sand, sniffled a few times, and using her freshly manicured nails, began scooping sand into the bags. Halfway through filling the second bag, a shadow enveloped her. Estelle looked up and squinted into David's face.

"What are you doing?"

Estelle shook her head. "I can't tell you."

"Why?"

"You'll kill me."

"I haven't killed you yet. In spite of fifty-two years of temptation. What makes you think I'd start now?"

She shrugged. "This is a new one."

"Ten kids, a dozen Chihuahuas, a house fire, and all the rest. What could be new?"

Estelle didn't answer.

"What's the sand for?"

"Kitty litter."

"You bought a kitten?"

"I packed the cat."

His brow wrinkled.

"Daisy?"

She nodded.

"Why?"

She tilted her head and gave him a dirty look. "I really have no idea how she got into the suitcase."

David stared at his wife for several minutes and then gazed out at the ocean. It was truly a gorgeous day.

"If I sit down in the sand next to you, I'll never get up again. How about we find someplace more comfortable and talk this over?"

"I think I'm stuck here," she groaned. "Can you help me up?"

"That'll be twice today, Estelle. You know, I'm keeping track."

Estelle reached up and David grabbed her hand. With a little effort, she managed to get balanced on her feet again. They walked over to the pool area and sat at a table under a large beach umbrella.

A waitress from the poolside bar came over, and they ordered a carafe of wine.

David looked at the two bags of sand in front of him. "Kitty litter, huh?"

Estelle nodded. "I already have the litter box set up."

"Of course you do."

"You're not too angry? I mean, we can't let anyone in the room or they'll kick all three of us out. No maid service, or room service, or fresh towels."

"We'll work it out, Estelle, like we always do."

His eyes smiled as he took her hands in his. "I just find it amazing that after fifty-two years of marriage you can still surprise the bejesus outta me." Then he reached over and planted a small kiss on her cheek.

"Happy anniversary, Estelle."

"Happy anniversary, David."

They lifted their wine glasses for a toast.

"May the adventures continue for another year," said David, grinning from ear to ear.

"Amen," whispered Estelle.

CHAPTER 20—BREAKFAST
AT HELEN'S HOUSE

Ruth held Ginger in her arms, rocking gently back and forth as her friend cried. Eventually, Ginger looked up, eyes red, nose dripping, jagged breaths. "Two years ago today I held my Leah in my arms and watched her slip away—my sweet girl. I know I'm supposed to move on, but I can't. Those last few hours keep playing over and over again in my head."

The ladies, for once, were silent.

"When does it stop hurting?" Her eyes pleaded for answers.

Bella spoke first. "It never stops hurting, my dear. But the pain does fade a little."

Ginger straightened, leaning back into the soft blue cushions of Helen's couch.

Ruth murmured, barely above a whisper, "Children are not supposed to go first. We're not built to handle it."

Bella resumed speaking, her voice barely above a whisper. "When I lost my Timothy, I thought for sure I would die. My world ended. But I didn't die. Time passed, others were born, life continued. The sun rose. You go on. Somehow. One foot in front of the other."

Ginger reached for a tissue and dabbed at her eyes. "Timothy?"

"My son."

"I never knew you lost a child, Bella. I'm so sorry …"

"It's all right. It was a long time ago … and it was yesterday."

Bella straightened her back, breathed in deeply, and exhaled. "Timothy was my first child. He was three years old. A cold, pneumonia, and two days later he was gone. He would have been thirty-five last month." She smiled sadly. "I still bake chocolate chip cupcakes on his birthday. They were his favorite."

"Daphne was only five hours old when we lost her," said Estelle, eyes brimming with tears, some falling, splattering onto the coffee table. "I don't know how one can become so attached to a frail little girl in only five hours. But we did. It felt as if we knew her for all eternity. And when she took her last breath ... what can I say? That's when David and I decided to become foster parents for other children with birth defects. Our first three were doing well. There was still room in the house … and a huge empty hole in our hearts. We ended up taking in seven more handicapped children over the years. It was the only way we could think of to make up for the loss of our Daphne."

Ginger reached out. Her fingertips gently wiped the tears from Estelle's face. "We've been close friends for several years now, and I never knew either of you had lost babies."

Helen reached over to put her arms around both of her friends.

"Amazing all the things we keep buried inside, things we don't share, until we absolutely have to," murmured Ruth.

"Talking about deeply personal things somehow never felt right ... or appropriate ... or safe ... or all of the above," said Ginger. "Not until I met you guys."

"Yes," said Helen. "Especially loss. It leaves you so unbearably raw. And most people really don't want to know. They have their own problems. Yet, sometimes sharing is the only way through the pain. If you have the courage to speak, and can find someone willing to listen."

Bella looked at Ginger and sighed softly. "You asked when it stops hurting, and all I can honestly say, is that time heals ... sort of. You do learn how to sing again, but there will always be a few high notes that you'll no longer be able to reach."

"We've all had losses," said Helen, looking around the room. "Some more than others. Parents, siblings, and friends are hard. Children are the hardest. But right up there on the grief scale are spouses. At our age, I'm frightened to think of the losses the next ten years will bring."

Ruth took a sip of coffee. "Life is a lesson of losses. You learn them one at a time," she said. "A patient taught me that, and her words stuck with me."

Bill's loud rasping voice startled the group. "What a glum bunch of kiddos you all are! Who died?"

All eyes turned to face him as he walked into the living room, tall, broad-shouldered, scarecrow thin, hauling a green oxygen tank.

"Bill," said Helen gently, "not a good time right now, dear." She started to tell him to leave, but Ginger interrupted. "It's okay. It's my daughter's yahrzeit today. She died exactly two years ago, and I was having a good cry."

"Oh. Sorry to hear that. You okay?"

Still clenching Ruth's hand, Ginger swallowed the lump in her throat, wiped her nose, and nodded. "I guess I'll have to be. How about you?"

"Still walking around," he said. "Beats being dead. This damn lung infection is putting up a good fight. I'm on my third round of antibiotics, which gives me the runs. So, I guess you could say I'm feeling crappy." Bill laughed out loud, and then began to cough.

Ruth looked at the oxygen tank and nasal cannula. "I didn't know you were on oxygen. Do you have to use it all the time?"

"Any exertion, like walking down the block, and I need it for the next several hours. But there are longer periods that I can do without. We're making progress."

Bella studied Bill's pale face. "If I was tethered to that damn tank, I'd be absolutely miserable. Yet, here you are, a really sick guy, and you look ridiculously cheerful. What's your secret, Bill?"

"Vodka." He grinned.

The ladies stared at him.

"Want some?"

"Vodka?"

"Put a splash of orange or grapefruit juice in it, and it's the perfect breakfast food."

The ladies watched him turn slowly and shuffle into the dining area, the oxygen tank in tow. They heard him cough a few more times before he called out, "Wow, this is some spread, Helen, and none of your kiddos ate any of it. You mind if I dig in?"

"Get the vodka first," yelled Ginger, climbing out of the couch and straightening her skirt.

"Okay." Bill laughed, coughed, and laughed again.

Bella reached for a box of tissues on the kitchen counter. "I've been going through an awful lot of these lately," she said, blowing her nose. "I need to buy stock in Kleenex."

"We all do," said Ruth, snagging a few of the soft white sheets and sticking them up her sleeve for later.

Bill opened one of the kitchen cabinets and pulled down a bottle of vodka from the top shelf. "Who wants?" he asked.

"Me," said Ginger.

"Us, too," said Bella and Estelle.

"Do you have any wine?" Ruth asked.

Helen went into the kitchen and returned carrying a bottle of Manischewitz Kosher Concord grape wine. "Will this do?"

"I'll take the vodka."

"I also have some cooking sherry, but it's a few years old."

"I'll take the vodka," Ruth repeated.

Bill lined up six glasses, poured a hefty shot in each, dumped in a few ice cubes and a splash of grapefruit juice, and passed them around.

The group gradually gravitated around the dining room table and began filling their plates: bagels, cream cheese, lox, brie, salmon quiche, stuffed grape leaves, herring in cream sauce, and homemade pastries.

Bill kept refilling the glasses with vodka while Helen brewed a pot of extra-strong coffee to sober them all up before they had to drive home. Then she checked to see if she had enough clean pillows and blankets, just in case none of them could make it quite that far.

CHAPTER 21—THE COCONUT BAR AND GRILL

"What the hell are we doing in this dump, anyway? I thought we'd agreed never to come in here," Bella grumbled, as she slid into a booth in the back room of the Coconut Bar and Grill. The torn red vinyl seat covering snagged her polyester pants with each shift of her bottom.

Ginger shrugged. "Sorry, my fault. It's so close to Dante's, I thought we could pop over and see how the construction was coming along." Ginger wedged herself as far back into the corner as possible. "God, this booth is small."

"Well, I think this was a nice idea," said Estelle, trying to adjust her skirt after shimmying across on the other side.

"Nice … shmice!" Bella snapped. "Dante's is closed, and the windows are blacked out. For all we know, the new owners are turning the place into a meth lab."

"Bella!" said Ruth. "What's wrong with you today? Why are you so grumpy?"

"Well, to begin with, my feet hurt."

"What else?"

"Well, I had a fight with Aldon this morning. I told him I wanted a divorce."

Helen's head snapped up. "What?"

"I told Aldon I was sick of him and I wanted a divorce."

Ruth turned to Bella and locked eyes. "What happened?"

"What happened? Oh, the usual garbage. But the way he answered me is the part that upset me most. He just looked me square in the eye and said, 'Fine ... I'll take the house.' "

Bella slammed her fist on the table. "Now, I ask you, what kind of cockamamie response is that? I mean, I could understand if he demanded reasons, or got angry, or cried, or threw something. You know, if he acted human. But to just say fine, no problem, we'll just divide up all of our stuff after forty-nine years of marriage and go our separate ways ... that is simply not right!" She threw her purse to the floor and using both hands shoved the table forward, pinning down her friends on the other side.

"Ow!" Helen cried, wincing. "Well, don't take it out on me!" Helen pushed the table back in place. "Do not shove this table forward again. I think you broke one of my ribs."

Bella growled.

"Ouch!" cried Ginger. "Someone kicked me. Was that you, Bella?"

"I think it was me," Estelle whispered. "I'm sorry. My sandal was falling off. I thought I was wedging my foot against the table leg."

"You mean he never even asked *why* you wanted a divorce?" asked Ruth, ignoring Estelle for the moment.

"No. That's the part that's driving me crazy. We went from having our multiple vitamins to splitting up the house, all in a minute and a half. He never even gave me a chance to yell and scream and tell him why I was so mad at him."

"Well, why *were* you so mad at him?"

"It doesn't matter," Bella harrumphed. Then she reached into her purse, pulled out several tissues, and wiped her eyes.

Estelle fidgeted in her chair, trying to look under the table.

"You're kicking me again, Estelle. What are you looking for down there?" asked Helen."

"I'm sorry," Estelle mumbled. "I was trying to find my sandal. It seems to have disappeared. I think it rolled under Ginger's chair."

Ruth tilted her head sideways.

"Bella, you two have been happily married for about forever. What's really going on?"

Bella sighed. "I don't know. I guess there are just some days I don't like him, that's all. I married this young, handsome, virile guy, and he's turning into an old fart. And I don't like it! I want to start over."

"Hey, it can't be any worse than what the rest of us are going through, can it? I mean, we're all aging," said Helen, reaching across the sticky table to stroke Bella's arm.

Ruth took out her bottle of hand sanitizer and began spraying the table. Helen wiped it down with some napkins.

"Yes, we're all aging, but I don't have to *look* at me," Bella continued. "I do have to look at him. Every day. The tremors, the memory loss, the bald head. He walks around the house belching and farting all over the place. And doctor visits, my God, we're booked from here to eternity!"

"Isn't there a book by that name?" asked Estelle as she reached down to scratch the big toe on her right foot.

"I think you need to get laid," said Ginger, looking around to see if she could catch the attention of the waiter.

Bella pouted. "Nice thought, but he can't even do that anymore, so getting laid is out of the question." After a moment of silence, her eyes brightened again. "Hey, maybe I should join an online dating service."

Helen laughed and clapped her hands. "What a great idea! That would be so fun, wouldn't it? To actually find out who, or what, is available, and if we're still marketable at this age."

"Wait a minute," said Ruth, suddenly energized. She began rummaging around in her pocketbook. "If you ever really decide to go through with that, I've got just the thing you're going to need!"

Bella craned her neck, trying to see into the depths of Ruth's purple tote. "What is it?"

"Here!" Ruth pulled out a photograph of a beautiful, young, raven-haired woman.

"Who is she?"

"Actually … I have no idea. The picture came with a photo frame I bought a while back."

"And you kept it because …?'

"None of your business." Ruth paused. "I liked her haircut, that's all. I show this picture to my hairdresser when I need a trim. Can't you tell?" Ruth shook her head slightly to fluff up her salt-and-pepper hair and tried to pose like the lady in the photo.

Ginger took the photograph and stared at it. She bit down on her lip to keep from laughing. "I don't mean to be cruel honey, but you don't look anything like the young chick in this picture."

Ruth's lips tightened. Ignoring Ginger's comments, her gaze shifted toward Bella. "So, do you want it or not?"

Bella looked up. "Are you talking to me?"

"Of course I am," said Ruth.

"I don't understand. What am I supposed do with that old photo?"

"Well, if you're going to sign up for an online dating service you'll have to provide a photograph. You don't want to submit one with what you really look like, do you?"

"Ouch!" said Bella.

"I didn't kick you, did I?" Estelle whispered, tucking her feet as far back as possible.

"Sorry," said Ruth. "I didn't mean that the way it came out."

Just then, the waiter — tall, black mustache, grease-stained shirt, — cruised past the ladies' booth. He dropped two menus on the table and kept going.

"Excuse me!" Helen yelled after him. "There are five of us here. Can't you count?"

The man snatched another three menus from the service desk and tossed them on the table in front of Helen, without saying a word.

"Thank you!" said Helen. "By the way, how's the food here?"

"Lethal." He sneered with dark teeth and walked away.

The women stared after him.

"This is not good," said Ginger, shaking her head.

"And his shirt was really dirty," Helen added.

Ruth starting gathering her belongings, "Obviously, this place wasn't such a great idea after all," she said. "Let's leave."

"Wait a minute, ladies." The booming voice emanated from a broad-bellied man in a red flannel shirt who rounded the bar and approached the table head-on. "Sorry about Carl. He's just coming off the night shift and is a little sleep deprived. The food here is actually top-notch, and we have great breakfast specials. Now, what can I get for you ladies?"

"Who are you?" asked Ginger.

"Saul Dinkman. I'm the owner." He smiled. "And you're Ginger Rosenberg, aren't you?" he said, staring at her red hair.

"Yes, I am. How did you know that?"

"We met at shul, last year during Hanukkah. We sat at the same table. You and my wife, Miriam, talked throughout the whole service. She wanted to call you, but she lost the paper with your number. She'll be so happy I bumped into you again."

"Saul! Of course!" Ginger flashed her professional social worker smile. "I had no idea you owned this place. How nice to see you again."

"How's Howie?"

"Um … Fine, thank you."

"To make up for Carl's fatigue, drinks are on the house," he announced while signaling Carl to drag over the easel with house specials scrawled in white chalk. "So, what would you like?" He rubbed his fat hands together and waited.

All eyes were on Ginger, who continued to smile tentatively. "I guess I'll try the number two special, Saul, with scrambled eggs and an English muffin instead of the home-fried potatoes. Oh, and for my free drink I'll have a double espresso."

"You got it! And what'll it be for the rest of you ladies?"

Ruth dropped her purple tote on the floor. "A Lantsman, in the Coconut Bar and Grill. Who would have guessed?" She batted her eyes at Saul.

After they ordered, Saul virtually skipped toward the kitchen singing Hava Nagila.

"So," asked Helen, "do you really remember him?"

"Not at all. Obnoxious little man. But I do remember the Hanukkah service and his wife. She was nice."

"So, I guess we're staying," said Bella.

"Yep. Seems so," added Ruth. "And, Bella, I am sorry if I upset you before."

"It's okay. Some days are preordained to be awful from the

start, and this was just one of them. I should have listened to my inner voice. This morning it clearly said either stay in bed or run away and hide."

"Marriage." Estelle sighed. "It gets better, and then worse, and then better again. A roller-coaster of compromise, my mother called it."

"You're right about that, dear." Ruth nodded in agreement. "By the way, did you ever find your sandal?"

"Not yet," Estelle replied. "But it's okay. I always liked going barefoot, and I'm sure it's under the table somewhere."

"Okay. Moment of truth," said Ginger. "Assuming that the food isn't lethal, and we all walk out of here alive, Bella, are you seriously planning to go through with this online dating thing?"

"Yes, she is!" yelled Helen, taking a paper napkin and wiping down the table a second time. "Let's do this together! I want to see what's really out there."

"You mean who …"

"Whatever."

Ruth snatched the photo of the beautiful dark-haired woman from Bella's hands, and shoved it back into her purse. "I'm in, but you'll have to come up with your own photograph now, because you're not using mine."

"Killjoy," laughed Ginger. "In that case, we may as well get back to dissecting the problems between Bella and Aldon. Did you guys ever make up?"

"Yes. No. Well, maybe to some extent. But then I left to

come here. There are still a few more things to hash out when I get back home. I guess we'll be okay. I just thought that after all these years it would get easier."

"How can it get easier? They're men!" Ginger snickered. "A whole different species."

A few minutes later, Saul and Carl arrived with the breakfast orders. Saul was smiling and babbling the whole time. Carl remained silent but was now wearing a clean, white shirt. When Saul wasn't looking, he reached across the table, handed Ginger a scrap of paper, and walked back into the kitchen.

"What is it?" asked Bella.

Ginger looked up, wide-eyed. Her lips slowly curved into a smile. "His phone number!" She laughed as she tucked the paper into her purse.

Bella chuckled. "Well then, I guess we haven't seen the last of this dump yet, have we?" Then she wiped her nose, crunched up the tissue, threw it on the table, and reached for a bagel.

CHAPTER 22 – MONEY TROUBLES

"I can't believe Estelle and David moved into this senior residence six months ago, and this is our first visit," said Ruth.

She, Ginger, Bella, and Helen met in the parking lot, entered the building together, and squeezed into the small elevator. Ginger turned off her cell phone, which had been vibrating all morning, and punched the elevator button for the fourth floor. As soon as the doors slid open, the group popped out to find Estelle waiting for them on the landing. She greeted them with an abundance of hugs and kisses before ushering them into her small apartment.

Ruth eyed the lacy white curtains, an overstuffed rocking chair, and an antique floral settee. "It's so nice to finally see where you live."

"Yes, it is. Your apartment is lovely! It reminds me of my grandmother's home," added Helen.

Estelle smiled. "I'm so glad you all finally came to visit. I know the place is tiny, but David and I are happy here. Mostly. It didn't make sense to stay in our big, old house anymore; too much to clean. Apartment living takes some getting used to, but it's near Alice. She likes to keep an eye on us, you know."

"Here, I have a present for you," said Ginger, pulling a brand-new lottery ticket from her pocket.

Estelle lit up with a smile broader than any Ginger could previously remember seeing.

"I don't know why you encourage her," sniped Helen. "It's such a waste of money."

"But it's her money," countered Ruth. "So what's the big deal?"

"Actually, when I buy my weekly tickets, it's with Dante's money, and they belong to all of us," Estelle rebutted.

"What do you mean?" Bella asked.

"Well … remember when I found that fifty-dollar bill in the ladies room, and nobody claimed it, and Roger said I could keep it? That's what I've been using to buy our lottery tickets for the last six months. The money only came to me because you guys let me go to the bathroom first. But really, it could have been found by any of us.

"I give up." Helen shrugged and walked away.

"I've got dibs on that rocking chair," said Bella, ignoring the conversation and trotting across the living room. She slowly lowered herself into the faux velvet chair, kicked off her shoes, and placed her stocking feet on a small rose-colored hassock. "Say, what happened to your geranium?" Bella lifted the lone plant from the window ledge behind her and spun it around. "The poor thing only has four leaves—which reminds me. Where's David?"

"Oh, David's got himself installed as the Grand Poohbah, or

something, on our resident council board. They've got a meeting this morning. It makes him feel important, even though he can't remember a damn thing of what goes on."

Helen's hand brushed the side of a burnished oak china cabinet in the corner of the dining area. She stared at the dinner service behind sparkling panes of hand-blown glass. "I don't know which is more beautiful, Estelle, this china cabinet or the dinnerware inside. I don't remember seeing either in your old place."

"We used to keep that old cabinet in the garage, but now that we've downsized and given away our big dining room set, we decided to use this piece again. It originally belonged to my parents. It's the last remnant we have of their furniture. And the china had been their engagement present to us back in 1959. It's Yugoslavian. Never used it much. Didn't dare with all our kids running around."

"The cabinet and the china are both exquisite," Helen said again. "What a wonderful gift. The only engagement present Bill and I ever got from my parents was a box full of fur coats."

"Fur coats? Plural? As in many?" Ginger was instantly alert.

"Yes. Two full-length coats, one ermine and one sable, and several mink stoles with matching hats and muffs."

"Now that I think of it," said Ruth. "I've never seen you wear any type of fur."

Helen shrugged. "I believe fur looks better on animals than on people. If you need to kill an animal for survival, I understand,

126

but for fashion, not so much. I just could never get myself to wear any of them."

"Ridiculous!" said Ginger. "It's not as if you ordered them. You got them as gifts. Done deal. Why not take them out for a spin?"

Estelle went into the kitchen and returned with a chocolate marble cake, which she placed on a small serving table. "Those coats must have cost a bloody fortune. Didn't your parents know how you felt about furs?" she asked, slicing the cake and doling out generous helpings to her friends.

Helen continued to stare at the oak cabinet. "I suppose so, but it didn't matter. They had no money, so they just gave us kids whatever they had lying around the house. When my engagement to Bill was announced, all they had was this huge box of furs, so that's what we got."

The ladies looked at her with blank expressions. Bella broke the silence. "They had no money, so they gave you a huge box of expensive furs? Are you kidding me? Where did they get the furs then?"

"Oh, my father stole them."

"What?"

"Didn't I ever tell you about my Papa Georgie? He was a thief."

The ladies all stared with blank expressions.

"The furs were his loot of the day. It could just as easily been a crate of tomatoes, or a pile of luggage." She shrugged nonchalantly. "Actually, I think I would have preferred luggage back then. Oh, well. C'est la vie."

Ginger blinked several times. "Your father was a thief?"

"Yep. Such a wonderful man! Even in hard times, Papa Georgie made sure we had everything we needed. He was such a good provider."

Helen's face melted into a sweet smile at the memory of her dad. Then she opened the china cabinet, and cautiously lifted one of the wafer-thin dinner plates. "Estelle," she whispered, twisting to face her hostess. "When was the last time you looked at these dishes?"

"Don't change the subject!" Ginger screeched. "I want to hear more about Papa Georgie."

"I don't know," Estelle answered. "David was the one who unpacked them when we moved here a few months ago. But it's probably been five years since I actually took them out to use. Why? Are any of them broken?"

"No. But there's a $100 bill stuffed between this plate and the one underneath it." Helen turned toward the cabinet again, lifted another plate, and saw the corner of another $100 bill. "Estelle, you've got money stashed in-between these dishes!"

Estelle put down a package of napkins near the cake platter and walked to the cabinet. "That's impossible," she muttered. "We don't have any extra money." She took the two $100 bills Helen showed her and stared at them. "Do you think the moving men might have left them by mistake when we came here?"

"Moving men putting $100 bills in-between dishes? Not very likely! Do you want us to look for more?" Helen asked.

Estelle nodded.

Ruth reached into the china cabinet and carried a stack of salad plates to Estelle's dining table. The other ladies quickly joined in, and within minutes they had cleared the cabinet of the entire set of Yugoslavian China. Sandwiched between each piece they found a crisp $100 bill.

Ruth and Ginger collected the money and handed it over to Bella. Bella stacked the bills neatly, and then handed them to Helen, who lined them up all facing the same direction and kept count.

Estelle's phone rang.

"Do you want me to get that for you?" asked Bella.

"No. I can't talk to anyone right now. I'm having a hot flash." She waddled over to the window and opened it halfway. Then she picked up the small geranium plant and plucked off all four remaining leaves.

"Check the soup tureen," called Bella. "It's in the corner on the top shelf."

Ruth, being tallest, was able to reach it. She carefully lowered it to the dining room table and lifted the lid. "Oh my God!"

"What?"

"There are five $100 bills in here!"

"And two hundred more in the sugar bowl!" said Ginger. "What's our count so far, Helen?"

"Sixty-seven hundred dollars."

"Yikes!!! Talk about winning the lottery! This is so much fun! Estelle, do you have *any* idea how all this money got here?"

"If it wasn't the moving men, then who else could have done this?" Estelle replied softly.

"There's only one person I can think of," said Ruth, turning to face Estelle. "It had to have been David."

Estelle slumped down in the floral settee and started fanning herself with an old copy of *National Geographic*. An amber-eyed elephant on the front cover seemed to wink at her with each wave of the magazine. She put the magazine down. "I think I am going to faint," she said. "I keep hearing chickens."

"Oh, sorry. That's me," said Helen. "I've been getting crank calls all morning. Give me a second, and I'll turn the ringer off."

Ginger scrunched her face. "You have chickens on your cell? Really, Helen, I am astounded by all the things I still have to learn about you!"

"Well, I found this great app of animal sounds for iPhones. I think it's cute."

"So, whenever we call you, we sound like a bunch of clucking hens?"

"Don't be silly," said Helen, tossing the silenced phone into her purse.

"The chickens are only for numbers I don't recognize. You all 'moo', like cows." She smiled.

Ruth went into the kitchen and returned with a glass of cold water. She sat down next to Estelle. "Here, honey, take a sip of this and try to relax. Just think, you are now almost $7,000 richer than you were an hour ago, and we haven't even checked the salt and pepper shakers yet!"

Estelle took several sips of cold water and poured the rest into the potted geranium. She sighed deeply. "David never did trust banks, you know, and that's the truth. His folks emigrated from Romania with only the clothes on their backs. They worked seven days a week to build a small haberdashery establishment on New York's Lower East Side, and just when they were able to rub two nickels together, bam! The Great Depression hit. His father's bank defaulted. They lost their home, and food for a family of six was virtually impossible to come by. David and his brothers still talk about the poverty of those days."

"That sounds just like our family's history." Helen nodded in agreement. "Papa Georgie's parents immigrated to the United States when he was only three. They were refugees from a work camp in the Ukraine, and also arrived at Ellis Island with practically nothing. The little money they had was used up within the first few months. His father eventually got work as a longshoreman, but was killed in an accident when Papa Georgie was only ten. At that tender age, Papa Georgie suddenly became the man of the house. Stealing was their only means of survival. He stole to feed his mom and the rest of his family. And as he got older, he got better at it. He met my momma when they were still teenagers and they were married when they were only seventeen.

Us kids came along pretty quickly after that. Stealing was the only thing Papa Georgie ever knew how to do. As a family, we were never rich, but Papa Georgie made sure we were never hungry either."

Estelle pried herself out of the floral settee and stared at the pile of $100 bills on the dining room table.

"After what happened to his father, David said he'd only keep a few bucks in our bank account to keep the government happy, and he'd take care of the rest himself. I always thought he was joking when he said he might stuff our mattress with it. I guess not."

"Should we check?" asked Bella.

"No! I'll talk to him later. On the chance that he did stash away more bills, I've got to tread lightly, so that he'll remember where he put them."

"Good decision," said Ruth.

A cell phone rang.

"Not mine," said Helen. "I turned mine off, remember?"

"Mine is off also," Ginger added. "Too many crank calls,"

"Don't look at me," said Bella. "I left my phone in the car. I think you win by default, Ruthie."

Ruth retrieved her phone from her purple tote.

She looked at her friends and shrugged.

"I don't recognize this number, but whoever it is has already called three times this morning. I think my hearing has gotten worse. I never even heard it ring."

"So, are you going to answer it?"

"Don't have to. Whoever it is already hung up. Oh, wait a minute—they left a voicemail."

She held up the phone and pressed the speaker button so that she could hear better.

"Hi, Ruthie, this is Josie. I've been calling everyone all morning. It's ten-thirty, and I'm over at Dante's having breakfast. Roger says you haven't been back since they reopened two weeks ago. Where are you guys?"

CHAPTER 23—RUTH'S JOURNAL #3

Our Anniversary

Awoke to sunshine streaming through the window. Gordon by my side. The usual good morning greetings after a 44 year love affair. We stayed in bed for an hour and a half, talking, cuddling. Comfortable. No back pain so far. Planning the day.

Phone calls from the kids. Three of four remembered. One actually sent a card.

A trip to town strolling through the Farmer's Market. Enjoying the fresh taste of honey from one of those honey sippy straws, and a wedge of warm homemade cheese bread. A steaming cup of coffee in hand. Reminded me of a Norman Rockwell painting ... Main Street USA. We bought a beautiful bouquet of orange and pink flowers, and two bags of fresh produce. Chatted with all the vendors we knew, then decided to go home.

I wanted to make soup with the new veggies. A huge pot. A 'Shissel' my mother would say. Plenty for us, plus some for a friend, some for my daughter, and enough left over to freeze.

It all went well until the freezing part.

I carefully ladled the extra soup into two 1-gallon Ziploc bags. Almost full when the wind, or my elbow, nudged one of the bags and it collapsed. A cascade of chicken/vegetable soup was suddenly pouring over the counter, sweeping a tsunami of carrots, celery, onions, and matzo balls in its wake.

Before I could right the bag, the culinary waterfall bumped its way down the steps of four cabinet drawers and splashed into an ever- expanding area in the middle of my kitchen floor.

I screamed.

Gordon came running.

He landed with both feet in the middle of Lake Chicken Soup, stared at me, and asked, "What's wrong, dear?"

I looked at him, pointed down, and screamed again—just in case anyone thought a loud wind was howling Saturday afternoon.

Time passed. About an hour. Working together, well synchronized after 44 years of marriage, the mess was wiped clean.

Gordon looked up. "How about going out for dinner?" he asked.

We did. Bought some expensive wine. Made a toast to years past and those yet to come. Splurged with chocolate lava cake and whipped cream for dessert.

"Happy Anniversary," said the hostess on our way out the door.

"Yes, it is," I replied.

Gordon put his arm around me and smiled.

A perfect day.

CHAPTER 24—HOPPING

Helen stared at the flotsam and jetsam of her life and tried to recall when her car last fit into her once cavernous garage. She peered out of the only window still accessible (the rest having been long buried under an avalanche of stuff), and could see her 1993 red Chevy Impala with yesterday's flat tire still parked in the drive. It had been more than a decade since her car had lost its home to her ever-expanding mountain of junk.

The junk will wait for another day, she thought. I am on a mission. The upcoming play date with her grandchildren frolicked across her mind. She located a clear plastic bin labeled *outdoor crafts* and reached deep inside with splayed fingers, hoping her sense of touch would recognize the item she was seeking.

She began to sing the twisted remnants of a half-remembered nursery rhyme: "Little Jack Horner sat in a corner, eating his pumpkin pie. He put in a thumb and pulled out some chalk and said, "Yay! I found it! What a great girl am I."

Helen giggled as she retrieved a fat piece of blue sidewalk chalk. She shoved a small end table out of the way and tossed a bag of empty soda bottles to the side, clearing a space on the garage floor. Then she got down on her hands and knees and scribbled eight large blue squares: Two connected squares, a third above them, two more connected squares, another single, and two more squares on top of that. Pottsy, they called it sixty years ago in Brooklyn. Hopscotch to her kids. *We played by the hour*, she reminisced. Hopping like little birds from one square to the next. Balancing first on the right foot, then on the left, while dipping down to pick up a stone, or two, or three, if you were a champion … which she was … back then.

"I will tear them away from their iPads and television, that's what I will do," she sang. "I will drag them to the park and teach them the games we played in the sunshine when I was a girl." She chuckled with delight. "It will be so much fun!" But she needed to practice before she could show off to the kids. It had been a while since she'd last hopped; a long while.

Helen placed her right foot in the first square, shifted her weight, and balanced precariously. She swung her arms back and forth, trying to gain momentum. Her right heel lifted half an inch off the ground, then clunked back down again.

"Well, that certainly didn't work the way it used to," she said out loud. "I'm not that old. I can hop. I'm sure I can hop."

Helen closed her mouth and tried again. She swung her arms more briskly this time, trying for liftoff. Still didn't work. Several more attempts proved equally ineffective.

"Maybe I can't hop anymore," she moaned, images of

showing off to her grandchildren rapidly fading. Her heart sank.

She caught a glimpse of her own face reflected in the shards of a fractured mirror hanging on the back wall. "Who are you, and what did you do with my hop?" she demanded of her reflection. Four melancholy eyes and six double chins stared back at her.

"Maybe you should start slower, with a small two-footed jump," answered her brain.

Helen took a deep breath, vigorously swung her arms back and forth three times, and on the fourth swing, leaped up with all of her strength. Momentum carried her a full inch into the stratosphere.

"See that, you old bag!" she yelled to the mirror. "I did it!" Then she took her pulse and quickly headed into the house to recover.

"Bill! Bill!" she called.

No response. Her eyes scanned the area. A note on the dining room table, pinned in place with a bottle of extra-strength arthritic-formula Tylenol, stated he had gone for a walk to the bank.

"Did you have to go now?" She crumpled the paper in her fist. "I needed to talk to you, Bill. I think I've lost my hop." Helen sniffled and threw the note back on the table. She tried to remember the last time she had jumped, skipped, or ridden a bicycle. Were those days truly gone?

The oxygen tanks, gathering dust, were lined up like bowling pins in the hall. It had been a tough year. She had almost lost Bill several times; her worst nightmare. The insidious aspect about endings, she realized, was that they sneak up on you. You never recognize that abilities, or people, are disappearing until they are already gone, or forever out of reach. She suddenly felt very alone and frightened. She wanted more than anything for Bill to hurry home and complete her world.

She heard the front door unlock and listened to Bill's footsteps walking toward the kitchen. He called out to her.

"I'm in the living room," she answered, brushing away a few stray tears.

"Better not say anything," said her brain. "He's got enough troubles without you acting like some crazy old bat. Keep it casual!"

Helen took a deep breath to calm her nerves. "You know, tomorrow is Wednesday. For the first time in months, all of us ladies will be meeting again at Dante's," she offered. "It's a whole new place now that the renovations are complete," she added nonchalantly.

"Uhm," Bill replied, picking up the newspaper.

"I've decided to ask the group if any of them can still hop."

"Okay," said Bill, shifting his attention to the financial page.

"That was a long walk. You feeling all right?"

"Uhm ... sure," said Bill.

She stared at him—a rosy color in his cheeks—no coughing. Oblivious.

Helen sat down in her rocking chair with a cup of herbal tea and hid her trembling hands. No cataclysmic losses this day, she sighed, just the hands of time slowly fraying the fabric of her life. Tomorrow afternoon she would try to hop again. There was still plenty of time to practice before the grandkids came on Saturday.

CHAPTER 25—THE HOMECOMING

"Good grief, they've painted the whole place red!" said Ruth, poking her head into the outer vestibule of Dante's Café.

Bella's mouth twisted into a frown. "A virtual sea of Campbell's tomato soup," she grumbled, stepping on Ruth's heel.

Estelle was next to squeeze her way into the small area. She ran her fingers along the uneven texture of the wall. "It's so bumpy."

"Campbell's soup with rice," Helen muttered under her breath.

"Well, they should have stirred the soup until they at least got all the lumps out," Estelle continued.

"I think they kept the lumps on purpose," said Ruth, draping her arm across Estelle's shoulders. "It's called texturing. It's supposed to make the walls look fancier."

"Well, it didn't work," belted Bella.

Ginger spun around, trying to get a better look at the ceiling. "Let's not jump to conclusions," she said. "Maybe that's only out here. C'mon, you guys, let's go inside and see what they did to the main dining area."

The group shimmied through a second door. Helen was first to walk across the threshold. "Red and brown stripes with gold zigzags? Really? What in God's name were they thinking?"

"And check out the window treatments," Bella added. "Red and green fringes on the shades. The place looks like a bordello. I should have worn my gold lamé dress."

Estelle glanced at the west corner. "Oh no! They've switched out our big square tables for little round ones. How are we ever supposed to push them together?"

Bella came up from behind. "And they replaced our nice soft chairs with little wire ice cream parlor doohickeys. My derriere will never fit onto one of those."

"Ladies!"

The five women whirled around in unison.

"Roger!" they shrieked with delight.

Estelle ran up to the 6'5" waiter, wrapped her arms around his waist, and began speaking into the middle of his chest. "I'm so happy to see you alive and well!" Her eyes filled with tears.

Ginger stood back, taking a longer view of her friend. "Wow. I can hardly recognize you in your new getup. You look so different in a red turtleneck. What happened to your old white shirt?"

"And why are you wearing an apron?" asked Helen. "You never wore one of those before."

"And what's with that letter *P* scrawled across your chest?"

grumbled Bella. "Roger starts with an *R*." She paused for half a second then continued. "Made in China, huh? They couldn't spell Roger, so they scribbled *P* for *Peeking*?"

Roger patted the gold embroidered *"P"* on the front of his starched black apron and glanced down at the ladies with laughing eyes.

"Ladies, welcome to Pierre's!"

Silence.

"Pierre's?"

"Pierre's," he announced again dryly. "Didn't any of you see the big orange sign outside?"

"Actually … no," whispered Helen.

Roger grinned. "So, how do you like the place?"

"It's hideous," said Bella, spitting into a tissue. "Why the hell didn't *you* buy this place? Then it would have been done right, instead of letting it be bought off by some foreign investor who turned it into ugly."

Roger tried to stifle his laughter. "Shh …" he whispered. "Believe me, I would have bought it in a heartbeat if I could have. But I'm glad to still have a job. Now, can you ladies please be a little quiet, just for today? It would really be best for all of us if the new boss didn't hear you. He's from Texas, and he thinks we got all fancy."

"But it looks terrible," said Helen quietly. "Surely he can see that."

"Not really. People see what they want to see. Right now,

let's just get you settled in with some breakfast, okay?"

"Is the food still any good?" asked Bella.

"Yep. Desmond's still here."

"Thank God for small miracles."

"That may be good for Desmond, but where are we going to sit?" Estelle wrung her hands and bit her lower lip. "Those little round wire chairs just won't do! I'll topple over, I'm sure I will."

Roger turned toward the back of the restaurant and gestured for the gang to follow. They did. He led them beyond the main dining room, around a corner, and down a short hall past the restrooms, where he pushed aside two heavy panels of red-and-gold drapes.

"Welcome to Pierre's banquet room," he announced apprehensively. "It was a last-minute addition when we were under construction. I managed to save these two tables just for you ladies, in case you came back."

The ladies stared into a small rectangular room with two square tables in the center.

Ginger leaned against the wall for balance while removing a piece of blue painter's tape from her shoe. "A little small for a banquet room, isn't it?" she said softly. "This space can barely seat the five of us. If Josie ever shows up, she'll have to sit across the hall on the toilet."

"I know," said Roger. "It was the best I could do. But there is room for expansion, and I'm still trying to convince the new boss to go for it." A half-hearted smile crossed his face.

Helen started to cough. "What is that awful smell?"

Estelle sniffed.

Ruth scrunched her face.

"It may be the paint," said Roger. "The men were here this morning putting some finishing touches on the ceiling. They weren't supposed to do anything to the walls, but …" He ran his hand along the red-and-brown boarder of the doorframe then looked at his fingers. "Oh, crap!"

"Oh, no!" yelled Ginger, jumping away from the wall. "Somebody look at my back! Did any paint come off on my dress?"

Ruth dashed behind her friend and began shouting orders. "Roger, we need a cloth and some water *immediately!* Don't worry, Ginger, it's only one little spot … or two, maybe three, if you count the edge. Anyhow, it doesn't matter—we'll get it out."

Roger dashed out to get a cloth.

"Uh-oh," Helen whispered to Bella, "Ruthie just slipped into her nurse-in-charge voice. It must be bad. You stay here and keep Estelle away from the walls. I'm going to get a closer look."

A half hour later, the five women were back in the west corner of the main dining room, awkwardly seated around two round tables, nibbling at the free consolation breakfasts Roger had brought them.

"This will never do," said Ginger, a beige woolen shawl draped over the back of her pale blue dress, which was still damp from its third scrubbing. "I am not going back into that little room ever again."

"Neither am I," stated Helen. "A person couldn't breathe in there. Banquet room from hell that's what it is. Dante's Inferno."

"I agree. It's a horrible, little room," added Ruth. "No windows or light. I get claustrophobic just thinking about it." She looked around the café. "After waiting so long for Dante's to open again—this is so disappointing."

"And ugly," growled Bella.

Estelle unscrewed the top of the salt shaker, dumped the contents on the table, and using her pinky nail proceeded to draw a sad face in the white crystals.

"So, what now? We're back to square one." Ruth propped her chin on her hands. "This is the only place we really liked that's centrally located between all our homes."

Bella looked at Estelle, unscrewed the pepper shaker, dumped the contents on the table and sneezed, sending a large cloud of black pepper billowing everywhere.

"Bella!" Helen snapped, "You just peppered my coffee!"

"And my pancakes," Ginger whined.

"Sorry," Bella muttered under her breath, trying to wipe the table clean with her sleeve. "Maybe we should try the Coconut Bar and Grill again. It wasn't too bad. Both the owner, Saul, and that waiter, what's-his-name, really seemed to like Ginger."

Ginger's face turned as red as her hair. "The waiter's name is Carl, and we are *not* going back there again, ever. End of discussion!"

The ladies looked at Ginger with wide eyes. Estelle stopped drawing faces in the salt.

"Why? What happened?" asked Ruth.

"Oh, my God," Bella chirped, waving her arms and smearing the pepper all over the floor. "That waiter, Carl, he slipped you his phone number just as we were leaving last time. You told me so yourself. Did you actually call him?"

"Start talking!" demanded Helen.

Ginger's face blanched deathly white. After a moment of silence, she stood, grabbed her coat, and made a beeline toward the front door. At the last second, she turned to the group. "You just wouldn't understand," she snapped. Then she ran outside into the rain.

The ladies sat in stunned silence.

The lines in Estelle's furrowed brow deepened. "What happened to Ginger?" She wrung her hands and began chewing her lower lip again. "Why did she leave?"

"I don't know," answered Helen, looking toward Ruth.

Ruth turned to Bella. "Are you sure about her getting a phone number from the waiter?"

Bella nodded.

"Well, something must have happened between the two of them."

"Something she doesn't want us to know about," Bella said loudly, dunking a paper napkin into her water glass.

"And we have to respect that," interjected Helen.

"The hell we do!" said Bella, wiping down the table with the wet napkin. "She's our friend. There's no privacy in friendships. I bet she's having an affair with Carl like she did with that guy, Jake in the bathtub, in Atlantic City."

"Of course there's privacy in friendship," Helen protested. "Don't be ridiculous. I don't tell you all everything!"

Estelle continued wringing her hands. "Helen, I'm getting confused. Was Carl in the bathtub in Atlantic City with Jake?"

"No, Estelle!" yelled Helen. "Jake in the bathtub was Ginger's first husband a long time ago. And Carl is the waiter from the Coconut Grill. Geez, Louise, try to keep up, would you!"

Ruth's voice was loud and sharp. "Helen, stop yelling at Estelle. She's doing the best she can. And Bella, what in the world are you doing?"

"I am trying to scrub the pepper off the table, so the next people don't think we're slobs."

"Oh for God's sake, Roger will take care of that."

"Well, then let's get the hell out of this dump," Bella grumbled. "This is the worst Wednesday I can remember."

CHAPTER 26—SECRETS

"Gordon!" Ruth stood at the bottom of the stairs and yelled up to her husband. "You promised you'd be out of here before nine. Hurry. Please. The ladies will be arriving any minute."

"I did have other plans for this morning, you know," he replied, slowly descending to the main level while slicking back his hair.

"Gordon..." Ruth snarled.

"All right, all right, I'm leaving. But I don't understand why everyone has to come to our house all the time. Why couldn't you just meet at Dante's?" Gordon grabbed the newspaper and his jacket, then turned and meandered back into the kitchen for one last gulp of coffee.

"We can't go back to Dante's until we hash out a few things. We need privacy, which means our house, which means you have to leave. Now!"

Gordon whirled his coffee mug in a large circle. "Big secrets, eh?"

"Yes," said Ruth, grabbing the mug from his hand and

dumping the remaining coffee in the kitchen sink. "Secrets. Now get out of here."

"Well, just for the record, I had other plans for this morning."

"Yes, you've made that abundantly clear."

"You'll owe me."

"Go!"

"Should I leave the nanny cams on?" He smiled nastily. "Then tonight the kids and I can heat up some popcorn and …"

"Gordon! Leave!"

"What about the hidden microphones I've got stashed in the lamps?" he added as he inched toward the front door.

Ruth snatched a large red pillow from the couch and threw it at him as hard as she could. Gordon ducked out of the front door, colliding with Bella and Estelle, who were just about to ring the doorbell.

"Ladies," he said, sliding by them, tipping an imaginary hat.

Bella stooped down to collect the red pillow that had landed on the front steps. "Is that man giving you trouble again?"

"AHHHH!!!" screamed Ruth. "He drives me crazy some days. "Bella handed the pillow to Ruth. "Next time, throw a brick. It works better."

Bella and Estelle walked into the living room and sat down.

"Is Ginger definitely coming?" asked Estelle.

"Yes," she said, putting a tray of cheese and crackers on the cocktail table near a full carafe of lemonade. "But I promised her this would not be an inquisition. So, Bella, pretend you're back in the library and whisper. And please, think before you say anything."

The doorbell rang. Ruth got up, welcomed Ginger and Helen, and ushered them into the living room. A somber minute passed before Ruth broke the silence.

"I would like to set some ground rules for this morning so that nobody gets upset." Ruth glanced around for objections. There were none, so she continued. "You ladies are the closest and dearest friends I have here in Oregon. But three years is not a long time for friendships to grow. Of course there are things we haven't shared."

Bella suddenly lurched forward in her chair. "Ginger! Are you having an affair with what's-his-face or not?" she blurted.

"Bella!" Ruth and Helen screeched simultaneously.

"What?" Bella shrugged. "I whispered, didn't I?"

Ginger clenched her teeth and glared at her friends. "No, I am not having an affair with Carl. Not that it's any of your damn business."

"Then why were you so upset last Wednesday at Dante's?" asked Estelle. "And why did you leave so suddenly and go running out into the rain?"

"Because I was embarrassed to tell you that I had called him."

"And?" asked Bella.

"And … we met, for a cup of coffee. That's all."

"But why?"

"Why what? Why did I meet him, or why was I embarrassed?"

"Either one." Bella leaned back in her chair, folding her arms across her chest.

"Damn it!" Ginger exclaimed. "Aren't any of you ever lonely? I've met all of your husbands and there are obviously issues with every one of them." Ginger deliberately stared at each of her friends hoping for some kind of reaction. There weren't any. "Aren't any of you tired of dealing with these declining men of ours, or with the thought of being caregivers for the rest of your lives?" She bit her lip and looked down at her feet. "Am I the only one who feels this is not what I signed up for?"

"No, you're not," said Ruth, hugging the red pillow tightly to her chest. "Life has brought so many changes in the last few years. A lot of stuff that everyone has to face, but no one seems to talk about. Yes, there are days I feel alone and overwhelmed. Too many of them, I suppose."

"I can bear the losses better than the isolation," Ginger said, shoulders sagging. "I don't understand why there's such a taboo against talking about the daily struggle. Sometimes I wonder if we even admit to ourselves how much baggage we've picked up along the way. How much harder it's becoming to carry it all. And all the while this conveyer belt called life keeps speeding up. Some days I feel like I can see the end coming ... and I'm not ready for it yet. I haven't finished living."

"I have something to say," Estelle interjected somberly. "As the oldest person here, I am very well aware that I am in the last decade of my life. Yes, the losses are mounting. They have been for some time: the aches, the pains, the hearing loss, the endless doctor visits, and on and on. So many of my women friends have been widowed in the last three years. I worry that at the end of my life I'll be alone. I don't know how I'll manage, or if my kids will just take it out of my hands and throw me into the closest nursing home." She paused.

Ruth leaned forward. "There's a saying: One mother can take care of ten kids, but ten kids can't take care of one mother."

"That's exactly what I mean," Estelle continued. "In some ways, aside from you ladies, I am more alone now than I've ever been. You see, David is not as sharp as he used to be. Well, that's an understatement. He forgets everything. No one talks about how to deal with a husband who is slowly going senile. No one. Not your children, not your neighbors, not your rabbi. No one. You're not even supposed to admit that it's happening, let alone tell anyone that you are having difficulty adjusting to this new person who needs you for everything. So, yes, Ginger, I know what it's like to be lonely. You put on a brave face and try to get as much as you can out of each day. What other choice is there?"

Helen started to speak, then changed her mind and reached for a glass of lemonade. A minute later she cleared her throat and addressed her friends. "I don't know what you're going through with Howard, and I'm really sorry about that, Ginger. But I've been the sole caregiver for Bill for the last year and a half. I won't go into any of the details …"

"Why not!" Ginger interrupted. "We're best friends! Why shouldn't we be able to go into the details? We've shared everything else. Why shouldn't we be there for each other where it concerns our husbands? If not us, who will be?"

"Do you really want me to tell you how often I had to wipe his ass or clean up his vomit?" Helen shrieked defiantly, her voice high pitched and quivering. "You want me to tell you about the times it got so bad this past year that I prayed he would die so he would no longer be in pain? And also, so that maybe I could get on with my life, instead of always catering to his constant needs? And I don't even know how to express the guilt I feel for feeling that way." She took a long jagged breath. "I did not sign up for this either. But this is where I ended up. And I guess this is where I'll stay until the ride's over."

"And kids …" added Estelle, "They don't want to know. Not really. We had ten of them, and they're all gone. Living their own lives. I know in my head that's a good thing … but in my heart, I gave them everything I had, and I expected to mean more to them than a once-a-week phone call when they are stuck in traffic."

"The hell with whispering. It's overrated!" said Bella. "I'm curious, what did Carl offer you that Howard didn't?"

"Love," Ginger replied stoically. "Not real love, of course. But I wouldn't want that, anyway. Carl offered me temporary love. Passion. Lust." Her lips curled into a wide grin. "Muscled arms … instead of withered limbs."

"You mean a good fuck!" Bella interrupted.

"Yeah. Well, we never got that far, but that was the offer."

"And you are considering it?" Bella asked.

"Why not? You were the one who wanted to divorce Aldon and join an online dating service a few months back. What were you looking for? A handyman?"

"Nope. A fireman," said Bella with a wide smile. "Have you ever seen any of those calendars? Humm!"

Helen laughed. "And what would Aldon say about that, I wonder?"

"Hey, he has his fantasies, and I have mine. The only good part about the essential tremors he developed lately is that he shakes so much when we get into bed it's like having my own personal vibrator. Puts me right to sleep!"

Ginger laughed out loud.

"That's terrible!" said Helen, choking back a giggle.

"Do you really have a calendar with firemen in it?" asked Ruth, grinning, "Because I may have to borrow it one of these days."

"Yep. I've collected them for years. And those guys are absolutely gorgeous. Kinda makes me want to set fire to my house just so I can get a closer look," said Bella, wedging a thin slice of cheddar between two rice crackers.

"I have a calendar of the Chippendales," stated Estelle, "and the men are mostly naked. I keep it in the top drawer with the monthly bank statements because I know David will never look there."

"Estelle! I'm surprised at you!" Ruth chuckled.

"Why? I'm not dead yet. And I love looking at their bicycles."

"Their what?"

"Their bicycles," Estelle repeated.

Choking back a giggle, Ruth managed to find her voice. "My dear Estelle, I have been a nurse for more years than I care to remember, but I am not exactly sure of where a man's bicycles are located. Would you mind pointing them out to me?"

"I don't know what's so funny," said Estelle, struggling to her feet. "We all have bicycles." At that point she made a little fist with her left hand, lifted her arm, bent her elbow to ninety degrees, and squeezed everything she owned. Using her right hand, she pointed to the spot between her shoulder and her elbow. "Aren't these called bicycles?" she asked, looking rather bewildered.

The ladies laughed so hard they could barely breathe. Helen snorted and farted simultaneously, which set them all off in another bout of hysterics. Ginger toppled off the end of the sofa and rolled, giggling, onto the carpet.

"Bicycles. Yes. I do believe that's the European term, dear Estelle. But here in America we call them biceps." Ruth fanned her flushed face with a napkin and then used it to wipe away the tears of laughter.

"Bicycles, biceps, whatever," murmured Estelle dropping into the couch. Her left shoe fell off.

"Forget the cheese and crackers, Ruth. I need chocolate and wine," said Ginger, climbing back onto the couch.

"In that case, follow me," Ruth stated, heading for the kitchen. The ladies re-settled around her breakfast-nook while Ruth ducked into the pantry. Moments later she returned with a jar of Nutella chocolate-hazelnut spread, five spoons, and three bottles of white Zinfandel.

"I haven't had so much to drink before lunch since last month at my house," said Helen after they had polished off all three bottles of wine.

"Weren't we drinking vodka at your house?" Ginger asked.

"You're right, so that didn't count. By the way, do you think Clyde has a brother?"

"You mean Carl?"

"Clyde, Carl, whatever."

"Could be. I could always ask."

"Then we could double date."

"Or triple, in case he has two brothers," added Ruth.

"Well, Clyde is not my type, and neither is his brother, if he has one," said Bella. "So me and Estelle are going to town on our own, and we're going to find some firemen with *big* bicycles."

"And will you remember what to do with them once you find them?" asked Helen.

"Well, if we don't, maybe they will," offered Estelle.

"And you'll report every detail back to the group at Dante's, right?"

"Pierre's," corrected Estelle.

"Well, maybe. Certain life events require a modicum of privacy, you know," Bella stated emphatically

"Wait a minute," challenged Ginger. "You're the one who insisted there was no privacy among friends. Just so you know, a complete report of any adventure will be expected."

"Sounds like a plan," agreed Ruth with a wide grin. "So the next question is … are we all okay with each other now?" Ruth asked, looking at Ginger.

"Yeah. We're okay. I do love you guys, you know." Ginger sighed heavily.

Helen tipped her empty glass over. "Of course you do. We're wonderful!"

"Yes, we are wonderful, but don't expect a report after my next date with Carl."

"Next date?"

"Oh-oh, …" Ruth took a deep breath, sighed, and then turned to leave the room.

"Where are you going?" shouted Helen.

"Back into the pantry, to find something stronger than this pissy wine. I have a feeling it's going to be a long afternoon.

CHAPTER 27—SARI
(Two months later)

Ruth blew through the front door of Pierre's Continental Bistro on an unusually cold gust of wind. She rushed past the main dining area, ran down the hall, and made a beeline for the newly expanded banquet room in the back where she sat down beside her friends.

"Sorry I'm late. I overslept," she announced, ripping off her rain bonnet. "Spent most of last night in the emergency room. Didn't get home until 3:30 this morning. Exhausting!" She paused for a minute to catch her breath while scanning the area for Roger.

"Can you get me a cup of coffee as soon as possible, please?" she called out the moment she spotted him. "Oh and forget the decaf. I'll need high-test to get through this day."

Roger smiled and gave her a thumbs-up.

"What happened? Are you and Gordon okay?" asked Ginger.

"Yes. It was my little granddaughter this time. Sari had another seizure." She sighed. "Gordon and I had just settled in for the evening. I was propped up in front of the TV with a hot cup of tea and a couple of chocolate chip cookies when Richard, my son-in-law, called us for help. It was just a little past nine. I tell you, no matter how often it happens, it is always unexpected. I flew out of the house practically without my shoes or bra."

"How many points would that be on Weight Watchers?" interjected Helen.

"What?"

"For the chocolate chip cookies. How many points?"

"I don't know, Helen. I'm not doing Weight Watchers."

Ginger turned on Helen with a withering glance. "Prioritize, Helen. That is not important at this moment,'" she snapped. When she turned back to Ruth, the expression on her face softened.

"She is such a sweet child," Ruth continued. "I got there just as the EMTs were strapping her onto the stretcher. She looked so tiny. It is absolutely terrifying."

"How old is Sari now? I've lost track," asked Estelle.

"Four and a half."

Bella reached across the table and pushed a menu in Ruth's direction.

"Where'd they take her this time?"

"Doernbecher Children's Hospital. It's part of the OHSU campus in Portland."

"This may be a dumb question," said Ginger, "but with all those people hovering around, what exactly do they expect you to do?"

"Just be there, I guess. They always call me. They even called when I was fifteen hundred miles away, visiting my son in

Virginia. But that's another story. Anyhow, when I get to their house, I pretty much follow orders. Most times they need me to stay and watch their other children while they take off to the hospital. Lillian always rides with Sari in the ambulance."

"Doesn't Richard go with them?" asked Bella, pushing a basket of hot rolls in her direction.

"Yes, though not in the ambulance. Sari is usually stabilized and discharged in four to six hours, so someone's got to follow the ambulance in another car to bring them all home again. This time, with the newborn being a bit fussy, they thought it best if Richard stayed home with the other kids, and they wanted me to follow the ambulance to Doernbecher. But of course that's when everything got screwed-up."

Helen looked up from her calorie-counting book. "Why?"

Ruth glanced through the newly installed windows of the expanded banquet room and watched several boughs of young sequoias stir the wind. She took a sip of hot coffee.

"I don't own a car seat the right size for Sari, so I had to switch vehicles at the last minute and drive Lillian's car because it had Sari's car seat already installed."

Ruth pulled a tissue from her purse and blotted the raindrops from her glasses. "I had expected the ambulance driver to wait for me. I had planned to follow him. Needless to say, he didn't wait. In the two minutes it took for me to switch cars, he sped off like a bat out of hell, sirens blaring, lights flashing."

"Well, getting Sari to the hospital quickly was his first

priority," said Ginger.

"I know that. Still, I didn't take that long. And trying to catch up with him at night in a pitch-black torrent of rain was impossible, and I ended up getting horribly lost."

"Lost, in the middle of a dark, stormy night, without shoes or a bra? Oh my," Estelle clasped her hands in despair.

Ruth tossed a vague smile at Estelle. "Don't worry. I *had* managed to get properly dressed before I left home. Been too well indoctrinated by my mother for anything else. My shoes and bra are attached to my driver's license, you know."

"Really?"

"No, Estelle, not really," several of them shouted at once.

"Doesn't your iPhone have a GPS?" asked Helen. "The new ones Bill and I just got actually talk to you. All you have to do is plug in the address and it tells you where to go."

"Yes, mine has that too."

"So?"

Ruth gulped down several more sips of hot coffee and wrapped her hands around the cup for extra warmth. "So … I was rushing so much that I stupidly typed in the wrong address. Who knew there were several places called Doernbecher? I had picked the wrong one. It was a dumb mistake, but there was nothing I could do about it at that point. Within seconds the idiot phone started yelling at me to turn around and head west, which I knew wasn't right."

"Couldn't you just pull over and change it?"

"That seems logical now. But at the time I was much too frazzled. And it was so dark I could barely even see the road, let alone change the settings on my phone."

"So you just kept listening to the wrong directions?" asked Helen. "That would have driven me crazy."

"In the beginning, the computer voice was okay. Like having a misguided friend for company."

"I know what that feels like," Bella muttered under her breath, her eyes flickering toward Estelle.

"I thought the computer would quickly figure out where I was headed and readjust the route," Ruth continued. "But she didn't, and as the miles passed, she got more and more insistent that I turn around. I tried to shut her up, but I couldn't find the off button. After fifteen minutes, I almost threw the damn phone out the window."

"That sounds just like my neighbor, Brenda," interjected Estelle. "A nice woman, but she drives me crazy when we go on trips: yak, yak, yak, from start to finish. There are times I want to throw her out the window, too."

"Well, I did eventually find my way to the Doernbecher Children's Pavilion. Only after all that, Sari and Lillian weren't there."

Roger came by with the breakfast orders. He cheerfully gave each lady her meal and brought an extra basket of warm crescent rolls, which he placed in front of Estelle, with a small plastic take-home bag. "Can I get anything else for anyone this morning?"

"No, thank you," said Ginger, smiling up at him. "But I must say how much nicer this banquet room looks now that you made it a little larger and added those two windows."

"That must have cost a fortune," said Helen. "I don't know how you ever convinced the new owner to do all this, but it's wonderful. And the new yellow paint reminds me of buttercups."

"So much better than that disgusting brown and red!" said Bella.

"Then it was worth the effort," said Roger. "I'm just glad you like it and decided to give Pierre's one more try."

"Me, too." Bella looked up from her French toast and smiled.

"Well, you can thank Miss Optimism for that," Ruth said, pointing at Ginger. "If she hadn't stopped by to get reimbursed for her dry-cleaning bill and told us about all the changes, we probably wouldn't be here right now."

"Yeah," said Bella, nodding. "I thought we'd never come back after that last time. Now, if you can just get that new owner to change the name of this place back to Dante's instead of stupid Pierre's, it would be perfect!"

"I'll try, but don't hold your breath." He laughed as he exited into the main dining area.

Ginger grabbed a crescent roll from the second bread-basket before Estelle could stuff them all in her take-home bag. "Okay, back to your story, Ruthie. What do you mean, they weren't there?" She reached for the butter and marmalade and put a large dollop of each on her plate. "Where were they?"

"That's a lot of points, Ginger," Helen called out suddenly. "Are you sure you want to eat all that?"

"I don't do Weight Watchers on Wednesday!" Ginger shouted.

"All right. Don't get yourself in a lather," said Helen, taking a tiny bite of her poached egg.

Bella turned to Ruth. "Yeah, where were they?"

Ruth gently removed one of the crescent rolls Estelle had stuffed in her take-home bag, smothered it with the extra butter and marmalade from Ginger's plate, and took a big bite. She carefully wiped her mouth with a red cloth napkin and swallowed another gulp of coffee before continuing.

"Well, when I finally got to the Children's Pavilion, only one curmudgeonly old security guard was on duty. He informed me that all ambulances going to Doernbecher at night don't actually go to the Children's Pavilion, but rather to the main hospital's emergency room which is located completely on the other side of the OHSU campus. No one had bothered to tell me that before. And when I asked for directions, it turned out that the nasty old fart had no more idea than I did as to how to get there. His only suggestion was that I go back out in the rain and walk up a hill. He thought I would probably find it in about twenty-five minutes if I stayed on the path."

"At night? In the dark? During a rainstorm? That's ridiculous!" said Ginger.

"What did you do?" asked Estelle. "I would have been

mortified."

"I demanded that he call a real security guard who could help me, someone who knew his way around the campus. After a bit of a fight and a lot of dreadful words, he finally did, and within five minutes a police cruiser pulled up, and this big beefy police officer got out and came straight at me. 'Are you the irate woman?' he barked, staring me right in the eye.'"

"I'm not irate," I replied near tears. "I'm lost! I just found out my granddaughter was taken to the emergency room, and I don't know where that is. And that idiot in there doesn't have a clue. Can you help me, please?"

"I think he realized pretty quickly that I was not some madwoman posing a threat to life and limb. 'Of course,' he said, softening his stance. 'I'll have you there in a minute.'"

He climbed back in his vehicle and motioned for me to follow. He was absolutely wonderful. Led me straight to the emergency room entrance, told me the best place to park my car, and wished my family good luck."

"And Sari was all right?" asked Bella.

"Eventually. Taking care of Sari is so hard. I don't know where Lillian gets her strength, or her patience. Sari usually recovers in a day or so. Quite honestly, it takes us a lot longer."

"Special-needs kids require a lot of love and work," said Estelle. "Of the seven special needs kids David and I fostered over the years, most were Down's syndrome babies, but a few had cerebral palsy like Sari, or had been badly damaged from abuse. They were all such wonderful children." A gentle smile blossomed across Estelle's face. "I loved every minute of being with them. But it was tough."

"There seem to be so many damaged kids now days. Have you noticed?" Ginger pushed her empty plate to the center of the table and brushed her long red hair behind her ears.

"We all thought we'd lucked out giving birth to normal kids. Who ever thought we'd be seeing so many birth defects in our grandchildren. That was just not supposed to happen. Our kids were all right, and their kids were supposed to be all right."

"I never even heard the term *special-needs children* until a few years ago," said Bella. "And now I have two nieces with autism and a grandson who was born deaf and needed a cochlear implant by the time he was a year old."

"I don't know if you guys remember when Josie's twin grandchildren were born—Pilot and Skye," said Ruth, "but the boy, Pilot, needed heart surgery when he was only three days old. And since then I've heard of a dozen other babies needing surgery for everything from closing heart holes to repairing intestinal abnormalities."

"None of us is untouched," added Helen. "Whether you're a parent or a grandparent, a neighbor or a teacher. My son, Jay, took after me and teaches high school math. The stories he tells are frightening. Half his class has to report to the school nurse several times each day for medication. Even at that young age, they have heart conditions, asthma, diabetes, and tons of behavioral issues due to genetic disturbances or drug addictions. And that's the new generation coming up. Our future."

"Scary, isn't it?" asked Ruth.

"Yes," said Helen.

"I'd still like to help children if I could. But I don't know if I can be of any use at my age," said Estelle.

"Well, the library is looking for some volunteers to help out in a preschool reading group once a month," said Bella. "You could do that."

"And there was also a notice in the local paper last week looking for folks to become Big Brothers and Sisters. Those are worthwhile organizations also," Ginger added.

"Oooh," said Bella, "I'd like to be a Big Brother!"

The ladies all turned to stare at her.

"What's wrong with that?" said Bella. "I get along better with boys.

"You can't be a big brother," Ginger started to say.

"Why not?"

"Don't bother," groaned Ruth, shaking her head. "But, switching subjects for a minute, I want to propose a special day trip for us; something different for a change, for next week. To lighten things up."

"What do you have in mind?" Helen asked.

"I thought it would be fun to spend a day at the beach, either Cannon Beach or Seaside. What do you all think? We could leave early, have lunch there, spend the day rummaging through the art galleries and stores, and still be home in time for dinner."

Just then Roger walked over to the ladies with a large platter of freshly baked cinnamon buns. "A present from Desmond," he said, placing it in the center of the table. "His way of saying thank you for coming back to us."

"Oooh!" said Estelle, lifting the first steaming bun off the top of the pile.

For the longest time, Helen sat back, watching the other ladies devour the cinnamon buns as they discussed the upcoming trip. Finally, when there was only one left, and it appeared Estelle was about to pop it into her take-home bag, Helen lunged and grabbed it.

"Points, Helen! Points! Don't do it!" her friends all screamed across the table.

Helen sighed. "You know, you guys are a very bad influence on my diet," she said, lifting the bun to her lips. "But apparently points don't count on Wednesdays; my best friends told me so. So I give up, okay?" She popped a very large chunk of cinnamon bun into her mouth and moaned with delight.

"None of Desmond's desserts ever have any points as far as I'm concerned," Bella stated, grabbing her spoon and scooping all the extra frosting from the platter. "And I agree, a trip to the shore is a wonderful idea. I vote for Seaside."

CHAPTER 28—A DAY AT SEASIDE

"How are you all doing back there?" Ruth squinted into the rear-view mirror and caught a glimpse of her friends in the backseat.

Estelle was in the middle, both hands wrapped around a half-eaten ice cream cone, melting chocolate dripping everywhere.

"I think we could use a few tissues back here," said Helen, sitting to Estelle's left. "Can you see if there are any in the glove compartment?" she asked.

"I'll check." Bella, who sat up front in the passenger seat, shifted her weight and reached forward.

"You might want to wait just a few seconds. The sign says rough road ahead," Ruth interjected, just as all four wheels of her vehicle took flight. Seconds later the car vigorously bounced back to earth again with enough force to propel Estelle's ice cream into her nose. One cold glob of chocolate landed on Ginger's leg.

"Ew! Need tissues back here, right now!" screamed Ginger, who was sitting to Estelle's right.

Bella hung onto her seat belt for dear life. When the car stopped jumping, she opened the glove compartment and began dumping its contents onto the floor between her legs.

"I don't see any tissues in here," she said as she tossed out a flashlight, two sets of earphones, a nasal aspirator, a set of Allen wrenches, two *Bon Appétit* magazines from 1986, one cracked sixty-watt light bulb, and a Ziploc sandwich bag stuffed with papers.

"Oh, here they are." Straining against the seat belt, she stretched her hand as far as she could reach into the back of the glove compartment. The shoulder strap pressed against her carotid artery, and her face turned purple as she fingered a small packet of Kleenex. "Agh," she groaned when her fingers finally closed around it.

"Be careful with those papers in the Ziploc bag," Ruth said, braking hard and cutting the wheel sharply to the right. Everything in the car shifted left. Including Estelle's ice cream cone, which landed on Helen's lap. "My registration and insurance information are in there," Ruth continued. "We'll need them in case we get into an accident." Then Ruth sneezed. The car veered right, then left, then right again before straightening out on the road, passing a double semi-truck with two inches to spare. "Oooh. Can I have one of those tissues please? My nose is itchy."

Bella bit her lip as she handed Ruth a tissue. "You're driving like a maniac! Can you please slow down!"

"Tissues!" screamed Helen. "Back here! Now!"

"Rest stop!" screamed Ginger, pointing at an upcoming rest area sign. "Over there! Now!"

Ruth steered the car off the main road and stopped. All the

ladies tumbled out of the vehicle. Ginger and Helen made a beeline for the ladies room. Estelle finished the last bite of her sugar cone and ran after them, curly white ringlets bobbing behind, half of them coated in chocolate. Ruth meandered to the edge of the overlook and stared at the valley below. The scenic overlook area was virtually empty—the view, spectacular. Only one other car, on the far end, was in sight.

"Can you feel that summer breeze on your face, Bella?" she smiled, stretching her arms up and out to the side and wiggling her fingers as if she were playing piano on the wind. "Isn't it wonderful?" She closed her eyes and took a deep breath.

"Don't lean so far over the railing, Ruth. You'll fall off the cliff," cautioned Bella.

Helen emerged from the bathroom and joined them. "No such luck," she whispered, "but we can always give her a quick push."

After using a full roll of recycled paper towels to mop up the final remnants of chocolate ice cream, the ladies prepared to climb back into the car for the remainder of the trip to Seaside.

"Lovely day," sang Ruth, tilting her face to the sun with a wide, relaxed grin.

"Yeah ... well, I'm taking the shotgun seat this time," said Helen, "so don't mess with me." She hoisted herself into the front passenger seat, climbing over all the debris Bella had thrown on the floor. She tossed the Ziploc bag into the glove compartment along with the light bulb and the Allen wrenches, which had somehow gotten stuck in the heel of her shoe. Then she kicked the magazines and other stuff further back under the seat and slammed the door shut. The door bounced open. She reached over and slammed it shut again. It bounced open again.

"Should we tell her?" whispered Estelle loudly.

"Tell me what?" barked Helen.

Ginger walked to the side of the car and lifted the seat belt buckle from the doorjamb. "Try it now."

"Oh," said Helen, looking down. "Thanks."

She pulled the seat belt across her lap and closed the car door. It stayed closed. "Let's go."

"But shouldn't we tell her?" whispered Estelle again.

"No," Ginger said, pushing Estelle into the backseat.

"Oh for God's sake, now what?" groaned Helen.

"Your sweater's sticking out, trailing in the mud," barked Bella as she buckled up in the rear.

"You know, Bella, you see very well for a person who needs cataract surgery," Estelle whispered.

Bella was thinking of how to respond, when Ruth peeled into oncoming traffic, singing, "Off we go, into the wild blue yonder." Bella and Estelle grabbed each other's hands and held their breath.

A few minutes later, Ruth checked the rear-view mirror and watched Estelle's face crumple into a frown.

"What's the matter now, dear? The ice cream was water soluble and easily cleaned up. No harm done."

"I know," whimpered Estelle. "That's not it. I love Darby's ice cream. I haven't had it for years. Thank you for stopping."

"Well, then, what's wrong?"

"Don't you think we should've called Josie to tell her about us going to Seaside?" she asked. "I'm worried about her. I don't want her to feel left out."

Ginger reapplied her orange sherbet lip-gloss and finished picking the pimple that had sprouted on her chin. "With all due respect, Josie hasn't joined us in months. I hardly think she'd notice."

"Has anyone heard from her recently?" asked Helen.

Silence.

"I guess not."

"I only need cataract surgery on my right eye," said Bella, sulking. "My left eye is still good."

Ginger spit into a used tissue and dabbed at her chin where the pimple had been. A tiny spec of blood was all that remained. "She was at least answering most of our emails for a while, but I haven't received anything from her in weeks."

"I heard she and Arthur have become good golfing buddies with Bert and Ernie," said Bella, waving at four handsome young men in a red corvette convertible.

"Who?"

"You know, Bert and Ernie—Mr. White Shoes and his fancy blond third wife with the drippy diamonds."

"You mean Albert and Ernestine Hornblower?"

"Yeah, that's them. Isn't that what I said?"

"Who cares?" said Ruth, flipping on the radio.

The sensual baritone voice of Elvis Presley suddenly flooded the car, demanding satisfaction from each one of them, at full volume. Conversation ceased. The ladies settled down.

Forty-five minutes later they arrived in the coastal town of Seaside, Oregon, and came to a stop, double-parked across the street from the Pig 'N Pancake restaurant. Cars were jammed in every visible parking spot along the narrow street.

Parents and children bustled to and fro on sidewalks, often popping out between parked cars to cross the road with little or no notice. Teenagers strummed guitars on corners.

"Wow, this place is crowded. Tourista heaven. Who would have thought so many people would be here on a Wednesday morning?" said Bella.

"Wednesday afternoon," corrected Estelle.

"Whatever."

"Now all we have to do is find a parking spot and we can get some lunch." Ginger unbuckled her seat belt and started gathering her things. "It's almost one and I'm starving."

Ruth's eyes darted nervously up and down the street. Her hands began to fidget on the steering wheel.

"Ooh," said Helen, "I see someone pulling out on the next block. Hurry up, and maybe we can grab his spot!"

Ruth shifted into gear and inched forward until her car was beside the vacant space. Then she shifted into park and turned off the ignition.

"What are you doing?" Helen cried. "You can't leave the car

double-parked out in the street like this. Pull into the spot."

Ruth turned toward her friends. "I can't." She frowned.

"Can't what?" asked Helen.

"I can't parallel park."

"Don't be silly," crowed Bella from the backseat. "Of course you can. Everyone can parallel park."

"Oh yeah, well, not me. I only pull into diagonal spots in shopping centers. I haven't parallel parked in years. And this space is so small, I just know I'll hit one of the other cars if I try. Can anyone else do it?"

"Don't worry about it. I'll give you directions," said Bella. "Pull up parallel to the car ahead of you. You can do this. It's easy."

Ruth pulled up.

"Now turn your wheel all the way to the right and start backing up."

Ruth turned the wheel and started backing up.

"Stop!" screeched Helen.

Ruth jammed on the brakes.

"You told her to turn too soon. We were about to hit the green car!"

"Okay. Everybody calm down," Bella ordered.

"Let's try this again … Ruthie, pull up to where you were before."

Ruth pulled up.

"Now turn your wheel and start backing up."

"No! She's got to back down a little more before she can turn the wheel and back up," argued Helen. "Which eye are you looking through?"

Ruth banged her head on the steering wheel in frustration, which set off the horn, which made them all jump.

"Oh God, this is never going to work," she moaned.

"Yes it will. Just back down a little bit further," said Helen.

"Turn the wheel now," yelled Bella.

"The other way," yelled Helen.

Ruth jammed on the brakes.

Estelle leaned forward and tapped Ruth on the shoulder. "I think you ought to pull forward again, dear, just to let some of these other cars pass by."

Ruth pulled forward again, parallel to the green car, and shifted into park. "Now what?" she sighed.

Ginger popped up. "I've got a great idea," she said. "How about if I get out and stand in front of your car and signal when to back up and when to turn?"

Before anyone could respond, Ginger hopped out of the car and walked to the front of Ruth's vehicle. They all watched her head spin this way and that, as if she were looking for something. Then her face curled into a smile, and she began waving her arms about in huge circles.

"I don't understand her signals," said Ruth. "What am I supposed to do, go forward or back?"

Bella rolled down the window. "Ginger, what the hell are you doing?"

Ginger's head suddenly snapped back to the car. She had a blank expression on her face. Her cheeks flushed. "Oh, I'm sorry," she giggled. "They're playing the score from *Phantom of the Opera* next door. I was conducting. Just for a minute. God, I love that music."

"That's it!" Ruth screeched. "Ginger, get your ass back in this car before I run you down."

"Well, you don't have to be nasty about it. I was only trying to help."

Before Ginger had time to refasten her seat belt, Ruth shifted into drive and took off, cruising two more blocks until the road ended. She took a hard right turn into the parking lot of the Shilo Inn. The lot was crowded. Ruth circled around several times and finally drove into the one empty, diagonal slot she found along a back wall, directly under a sign that said *For Hotel Guests Only.* She turned off the ignition and picked up her purse.

"Are we allowed to park here?" asked Estelle.

"We're staying."

Helen got out and stretched. She reached over to help Estelle. "Look at the bright side, honey, by the time they discover us we'll be gone. And in the meantime, we're practically on the promenade, so you won't have to walk very far."

"I guess that's good," said Estelle as she lurched onto her feet. She held onto Helen for support for several seconds until she got her balance. "And the hotel probably has bathrooms. I've really got to pee."

"Again? We've already stopped three times for you. Is something wrong?" said Ruth.

"Don't you just love *Phantom of the Opera*?" said Ginger.

"I wonder if Josie can parallel park," said Bella.

"Of course they have bathrooms," said Helen.

"I'm getting old," said Estelle.

The five of them unfurled their bodies and waddled toward the hotel's front door.

Twenty minutes later they were walking down the block headed toward the Pig 'N Pancake restaurant. The sun was bright, the air brisk, and their walk slow, as they stopped to look in many of the shops en route.

"Come on, guys, we can see all this on our way back to the beach after lunch," said Ruth. "I'm really hungry and desperately in need of a cup of coffee."

"Oooh," said Ginger, "I see something in this next store that I want. You guys go ahead, and I'll catch up in a minute." Ginger peeled off and ducked into one of four connected gift shops. By the time she caught up with her friends, they were already seated in the restaurant, laughing so loudly they could be heard across the entire dining area. She scooched in beside them, a small, brown, paper-bag now sticking out of her pocketbook.

"So, what'd I miss?"

Ruth pushed a glass of ice water her way and pointed to the

senior section on the menu. "Estelle was entertaining us with how many times a night she's got to run to the bathroom, and how the medicine to control it is making her loopier than normal." They all giggled.

"And I was telling them how many hours I spent on the phone last week with the poison control center, when Aldon accidentally took all of my medication instead of his own," added Bella.

"Time to order," said Helen. "Here comes our waiter."

"Oooh. Did we get the cute one?" asked Ginger with a smile.

"Yes, we did. His name is Jason. Now, stop ogling and look down at the menu."

"He's adorable," said Estelle. "Eye candy, just like Roger."

"Eye candy and incontinence don't mix," whispered Ruth.

Estelle pouted.

Jason walked up to their table and took out his order pad. "You ladies ready to order yet?"

"Yes. I think so." Ruth handed him her menu. "I'd like ..."

"I'll have the number two senior breakfast special with poached eggs and rye toast," interrupted Bella.

"Hash browns or French fries?"

"Can I have fruit instead of the potatoes?"

"Sure."

Jason turned to Estelle. "And what would you like?"

"I'll have one pancake and one egg."

"How do you want the egg?"

"I don't really want the egg. On second thought, maybe I'll

just have two pancakes this morning."

"Okay."

Bella waved her hand. "I changed my mind. Can you give me scrambled eggs instead of poached?"

"Can do." Jason rewrote the order.

"And change my fruit salad back to hash browns, okay?" added Bella.

"And can I have chocolate chips in my pancakes?" asked Estelle.

"Certainly. The pancakes also come with a side of bacon or sausage."

"Oh, I don't want the bacon."

"Don't listen to her," said Ginger. "I'll take her bacon."

"Okay," said Estelle.

"But make it well done and crispy."

"Got it. Well done and crispy," repeated Jason.

"Do you want anything else with that?" he said, looking at Ginger.

"Yes. Hmm. I think I'll have a cheese omelet, and a fruit salad."

"Okay."

"And the bacon."

Bella waved her hand again. Jason looked up. "Could you add a side of bacon for me too? That sounds really good."

"Sure thing." He scribbled more notes in his order pad.

"And can you make my cheese omelet with only two eggs instead of three?" asked Ginger. "I've got borderline high cholesterol."

"I've got to check with the cook on that, but I'm pretty sure he can do it."

"How's your corned beef hash?" asked Helen.

"Really good," said Jason. "You want fries with that?"

"No, I just wanted to know how it was. I'm going to have the eggs benedict. And do you have Jell-O?"

"Yes ma'am. Strawberry or lime?"

"I'll take the French fries."

"No Jell-O?"

"No Jell-O."

"Hmm," muttered Jason. "French fries. Got it."

"And I'll have the number four special," said Ruth. "Scrambled eggs, home fries, soft bacon, and a dry English muffin."

"Remember," interjected Ginger, "her bacon is soft, and mine is well done and crispy."

"And mine can be medium," said Bella.

Jason refilled their coffee mugs, scribbled down a few more changes, and left with their orders.

"You know something, Estelle. I think you were right. He is every bit as cute as Roger. Just a little younger."

"And he did have very big bicycles," Bella posed with her arm muscles flexed, and grinned.

"Yes, but did they look bigger with your right eye or your left eye?" Estelle laughed.

Ignoring Estelle's comment, Bella turned toward Ginger. "So, what'd you buy?"

Ginger removed the brown paper-bag from her purse and placed her purchase on the table.

Silence.

"What? Nobody's going to say anything?"

"I'll say something," said Bella. "You're crazy!"

"Why? It's adorable!"

"A yellow rubber ducky in a raincoat? Really? What the hell are you going to do with that?"

"I don't know," Ginger frowned. "He just looked so cute."

Ruth sighed. "Okay, he is cute. It's just that you've been complaining that your house was getting very crowded, and you were afraid you were turning into one of those hoarder ladies, like on TV. Did you really need to buy a rubber duck?"

"Yes," Ginger replied firmly. "To add to my collection."

"You have a collection of rubber ducks?"

"Yes. I've named this one Murphy."

Helen rolled her eyes.

"Come to think of it, my uncle Seymour had a raincoat just like that," said Bella. "And he was the same color yellow that year he had hepatitis."

"Time-out. Here comes Eye Candy with our food," said Estelle, licking her lips.

Halfway through the meal, Ruth stared across the table. "Helen?"

"Yes?"

"Why are your hands shaking?"

Helen stopped eating and folded her hands in her lap.

"I'm sorry," said Ruth. "I didn't mean to embarrass you."

Helen took a deep breath and sighed. "Is it that noticeable?" she asked.

"Maybe just today."

"It's the same thing Bella's husband has. It's called essential tremors. It doesn't kill you—it's just there. I don't know how long Aldon has had it, but mine started gradually a couple of months ago. One of those genetic things. A gift from my mom."

"Can they do anything about it?"

"Pills, and more pills. I'm sure I'll find a silver lining for it if I look hard enough."

"I know," said Estelle, brightening up. "As long as it doesn't kill you, maybe the shaking will help you lose some weight!"

For some reason the people at the next table thought that was very funny and started laughing.

"Time to hit the beach," said Bella. "Finish up, and let's go. The sky is beginning to cloud over."

The ladies gobbled down their last bites and took turns going to the bathroom, while Jason processed all five credit cards.

They held one final summit meeting, directed by Helen, to arrange an equitable tip with all bills facing the same direction, before they trotted off to see the ocean.

The stroll back to where the sand and promenade began, took a half hour. During that time, Ginger managed to buy a pink Seaside sweatshirt, a pair of seashell salt and pepper shakers, and a wood treasure chest large enough to hold the purple iridescent Yo-Yo she had purchased earlier.

Helen, Ruth, and Bella began their trek in the sand, while Ginger stored her loot in the trunk of the car, and Estelle ran into the Shilo Inn again for one more pit stop.

Ruth stared at the waves and kicked some sand around, waiting for the others to catch up.

"What's the matter, Ruthie?" asked Helen. "A minute ago you were all bouncy, and now you seem as deflated as the weather."

"Oh, it's nothing terribly important. I was just asked to write an article on the joys of aging for our sisterhood journal. It's due Friday, and I haven't done it yet."

"Why not?"

"I dunno."

"Not so much joy, huh?"

"Not always, that's for sure. When I agreed to write the article it seemed like such a good idea, but now, I can't come up with one coherent thought. Lots to ponder."

"Well, maybe you should just turn it over to someone else," said Bella.

"No. I still want to do it, or at least a part of me does."

"Do you want me to find some good library books for you on writing techniques for retired nurses on pensions? I've still got some connections at the Beaverton branch, you know."

"Thanks, Bella, but I'll pass on that. I just need a few minutes of solitude, so my thoughts can coagulate. I think I'll just climb over that sand dune and commiserate with the ocean a bit."

Ruth kicked off her sandals, threw them in her purple tote, and headed for the water's edge.

"That's hardly a sand dune," Helen called after her. "More like the squished-up edge of a tire track."

"Aargh!" said Ruth, as she trotted off, leaving the rest of the group behind.

"What now?" asked Helen.

"Time for fun! The last one to dunk their feet in the water is a rotten egg," Bella yelled. Then she ran off as fast as she could with Ginger, Helen, and Estelle scurrying quickly behind.

Twenty minutes later, all five of them were together again at the water's edge building a mammoth sand castle and intermittently splashing each other.

"It's going to rain soon," said Ruth.

"I hope it can hold off for one more hour," said Helen, wiping away the first small raindrop that landed on her nose.

"I've got one! I've got one!" squealed Estelle, who had plopped herself closest to the surf.

"What did you get?" Ginger leaned over to inspect the

contents of Estelle's cupped hands.

"It's a sand crab," squealed Estelle again in a delighted little girl voice. "I haven't caught one of these since forever ago!"

"Well, what are you going to do with it?"

Estelle licked her lips.

"Are you going to eat it?" asked Ginger, sticking out her tongue as if trying to spit out a fly.

"No! You don't eat them. You let them go, then try to catch another. It's all about the conquest!"

"Have you noticed how dark the clouds are getting?" asked Ruth. "We better get out of here." Just as she finished speaking, the sky opened up, and a torrential rain poured down upon them.

"Goodbye, little sand crab," said Estelle, tossing the tiny animal back into the sea.

The five ladies gathered their belongings and ran back to the Shilo Inn where they dried off as best they could in the ladies' room.

"Time to go home?" Ruth asked.

'Yes', they all nodded. "But first, let's stop in the hotel coffee shop and order an afternoon snack and some hot drinks," said Bella, using her floral silk scarf to wipe the sand from between her toes. "Maybe we can do this again soon. This was really nice."

"I agree," said Helen. "The fresh salt air, walks along the beach, a full day mostly in the sun. It was wonderful."

"The best day I've had in a month," smiled Estelle, looping her arm through Ruth's. "Thank you so much for suggesting this."

"Yes, it was a nice day, wasn't it," said Ruth. "And I think I figured out what I want to say in my article, *'The Joys of Aging.'* I'll tell you all about it on the way home."

"Ooh," said Estelle. "Are we in it?"

"Absolutely!" answered Ruth.

Ginger waved her hand around. "I've got the shotgun seat on the way back!" she called racing toward the front passenger seat.

It was five o'clock when they all piled into Ruth's old car, realized they had a flat tire, and ran back to the Shilo Inn to call the AAA.

CHAPTER 29—HOWARD

The waiting room was small and smelled of antiseptic spray. Two rows of threadbare blue chairs lined the back wall. Ruth stopped pacing and sat down. She looked at her watch for the third time. 9:05 p.m. "I feel like we've been here for hours."

"Nope. Only forty-five minutes." Helen sighed. "Do you think they will let us see him?"

The over-head speaker blared, causing both ladies to jump. "Dr. Reading, call extension 907, Dr. Reading, extension 907." Then it went silent.

"I guess it depends on how bad off he is." Ruth spoke in her professional nurse voice.

Sliding glass doors at the end of the gray corridor yawned open. Estelle and her daughter, Alice, whisked through the emergency room entrance, blown in on a heavy night wind.

"We got here as soon as we could." Estelle shivered. "What have you heard?"

"Nothing much," said Ruth. "Ginger popped her head out about a half hour ago to fill us in and then ran back inside."

Estelle pulled off her wool sweater, folded it neatly, and draped it over the back of the closest chair. "You both remember my daughter, Alice, don't you?" The ladies nodded and greeted her. "She wouldn't let me drive here alone in the dark."

"Of course I wouldn't," said Alice. "So what's the latest on Howard? What exactly did she say?"

"They're still working on him. They think he's had a stroke."

The glass doors at the end of the hall slid open again, and Bella hobbled in, lumbering under the weight of an infant carrier. She was flushed and sweaty and looked as if she were about to pass out. The group ran to assist her. Alice took the carrier from her and brought it over to the main waiting area. "My God, is this little Bojo?"

"Yes. I was babysitting tonight," Bella puffed. "Bonnie and Joe went to the movies. It was supposed to be a quiet night. Ha!"

"Come over here and sit down," Ruth ordered, "before you have a stroke too."

Bella, still short of breath, nodded and sat down in the first available chair, landing on top of Estelle's sweater.

"Look how big he's gotten! How old is he now?" Helen leaned over the infant carrier and pinched the baby's cheek.

Bojo opened his eyes, took one look at Helen, and screamed at the top of his lungs.

"Oh, great," Bella grumbled, trying to pull herself out of the chair. "You just had to wake him, didn't you?"

"Stay still." Estelle pointed at Bella. "I've got this." She lifted the baby out of the carrier, swaddled the blankets around his little body, and began cooing at him as she danced around the waiting room. Bojo stopped crying, closed his eyes, and went back to sleep.

"How'd you do that?" Bella whispered.

"Easy. I'm good with babies," said Estelle as she returned Bojo to the infant carrier and moved it away from Helen.

"He's nine months old," sighed Bella, "and most of the time he's an absolute terror. The next time I'm recruited to babysit I may have to hire you."

"Okay, but I'm not cheap."

Ruth smiled. "Oh yeah? What's your price?"

Estelle scratched her chin pensively. "Well, let's see. For one absolute terror, I'd have to charge at least two milk chocolate Hershey bars."

The treatment door opened and Ginger walked into the waiting area. The ladies ran toward her, trying to read the expression on her face.

"It's not a stroke," she said, barely above a whisper. "He forgot to take his medications again today, and when his blood pressure dropped, he passed out."

She started to sway. Helen grabbed her elbow and steadied her.

"You need to sit down," she ordered.

The ladies cleared a space in the cluster of chairs they

occupied and gathered around.

"Can we get you anything?" Ruth asked. "Some juice, tea, a sandwich from the coffee shop?"

"No, thank you. I really don't want to stay out here too long. The doctors are in with Howard now, but they'll be finished soon, and he's afraid of being alone."

"What else did they tell you?" asked Alice. "And what can we do to help?"

"There is nothing to be done yet, at least not until all the test results are in. The first thing they're checking out is his head. He clunked it pretty hard on the kitchen counter when he fell, and he's got a nasty gash. They think he might have a concussion. And then there's his hip. That's where he landed, on his left hip. The ER doctor is pretty sure it's broken. They sent him for an X-ray about an hour ago, and we're waiting for the orthopedist on-call to arrive to tell us for sure. The big question is whether or not he will need surgery." She took a deep breath. "And they also have a call in to his cardiologist. This hospitalist is very thorough. He wants to make sure that Howard doesn't have any kind of heart blockage, which could have contributed to his passing out."

Estelle nudged closer to Ruth. "What's a hospitalist?" she asked.

"In the old days, your personal doctor followed you when you went into the hospital and he cared for you during your entire stay," Ruth explained. "But in this new world of ours, *they*, meaning the insurance companies, decided that was not a fiscally efficient plan. So now there are doctors that only work in the hospitals, and they take care of you, start to finish, during the entire time you're admitted. They call themselves Hospitalists."

"So your own doctor, the guy who knows you best, is not in charge of your care anymore?"

"Nope. Not when you're in the hospital." Ruth shrugged. "That's just how it is."

Ginger rubbed her eyes and yawned. "Sorry. I'm exhausted." She pushed a few strands of long, stringy red hair behind her ears and yawned again. "Well, our regular doctor retired last year," she said, "and so many of the doctors in our area are no longer accepting older people with Medicare. It's disgusting. I'm just glad we were able to find any doctor to care for us. This one speaks English and seem really nice, so I'm not complaining."

Just then Bojo opened his eyes and cried.

"You brought the baby here?"

"Yeah," said Bella. "I was babysitting and I couldn't leave the little guy home alone. Although I was tempted."

Ginger knelt in front of the infant seat and tickled Bojo's chin. The baby smiled and cooed. "I can't tell you how much I appreciate everyone being here," she said, looking up, "but it's late, and God only knows how much longer this is going to take. You guys really ought to go home. I'll be all right. Really."

"Well, I'm staying," said Ruth. "At least until some of those test results come in."

"Me too," added Helen, inching closer to the baby carrier.

Bojo took one look at Helen and screamed.

Prying herself out of the chair, Bella skulked over to her grandson. "Oh for God's sake, stop it, Bojo! And you, Helen, stay away from the kid. Can't you see he hates you?"

Helen pouted and walked away. Bojo kept screaming. Estelle grabbed another blanket from the diaper bag and wrapped it snuggly around Bojo's belly. He looked at Estelle, stopped crying and began to giggle.

"That's it," said Bella. "You're coming home with me."

Just then one of the nurses called to Ginger, and she went flying back toward the treatment area. "Really, guys," she called over her shoulder, "thank you so much for coming, but it's late. Go home. I promise I'll call you as soon as I have any news." Ginger slipped through the door that led to the treatment area and was gone.

After a brief discussion, Estelle, Bella, and Alice, carrying Bojo, gathered their stuff and left. Helen and Ruth settled in for a long night; Ruth with her current mystery novel and Helen with her latest crossword puzzle.

At seven the next morning, Howard was wheeled into surgery for a total hip replacement. At noon the hospital social worker presented Ginger with all the documents and consent forms necessary to send him to a rehab facility once he was deemed medically stable.

CHAPTER 30 —PHONE CALLS

Day I

Thursday morning

Ginger to Ruth:

"Hi, Ruth. Yes, we're doing okay. The doctor came out a few minutes ago and said the surgery went well ... No complications, so far ... Yes, he's in recovery. They did what they called a *total hip* ... I have no idea if it was an anterior or posterior approach. I don't even know what that means ... I don't really care. Just tell the others we're okay. I gotta go."

Thursday afternoon

Estelle to Ruth:

"Ruthie? ... Thank you for letting me know ... No, don't worry so much, I am not short of breath. Our mail pickup is early, and I just ran out to get something in the mailbox before the mailman arrived, that's all ... Well, I wanted to send a note to Ginger as soon as possible. Luckily, I found an unused birthday card in my desk ... Don't be silly, of course I scratched out the birthday part. Actually, I covered it in white-out, and when it dried I wrote *condolences* in big letters all across the top and then signed all our names … Oh my God! Ruthie! You're right! He didn't die! I should have written *get well*! Oh, Ruthie, what should I do? I've just sent out so many condolence cards lately it was sort of automatic … Do you think if I stood by the mailbox the mailman would let me take it back again?"

Day 2

Friday late morning

Ginger to Bella:

"Yes, Bella, I hear you, please stop shouting. No, I don't need any library books. Yes, he's still sleeping a lot … I have no clue how many stitches he has; he's all bandaged up. Why does that matter? … Well, I don't believe in numerology … Okay, I promise the next time he wakes up I'll ask if he wants a book … Yeah, I'm okay, but getting a little worried. Honestly, he seems a bit confused … I'll be meeting with the social worker this afternoon to talk about rehab centers … Tomorrow, I think … I really don't understand why they have to push him out of the hospital so quickly. I'm not sure he's ready. I know I'm not."

Friday afternoon

Ginger to Helen:

"Stop! You are the third person today to tell me about someone who died from blood clots after hip surgery. I don't want to hear it anymore, okay? … No, Helen, what you and Bill went through last year was completely different. I'm struggling to stay positive about all this, and all these doom-and-gloom stories don't help. I gotta go."

Day 3

Saturday early

Estelle to Ruth:

"Ruthie? Have you spoken to Ginger today? She sounds awful. I really don't understand the medical world these days. You mean the only rehab place that would accept him is all the way down in Salem? That's more than an hour's drive from her house! No wonder she's a mess. What can we do to help? … Well, as soon as you think of something let me know ... You know, my neighbor died of a blood clot a month after his hip surgery, do you think I should tell her about it? … All right, all right, stop yelling. I promise I won't say a word."

Day 4

Sunday morning

Bella to Helen:

"Hi, Helen. Are you busy today? … I know it's Sunday, but I was thinking of taking a ride down to that rehab place in Salem to visit Ginger and Howard, and I was wondering if you wanted to come along … No, you're the first one I called … Okay, you call Estelle, and I'll call Ruth …What kind of pie? Ooh, peach is my favorite … Okay, you bring the pie, and I'll bring some library books. I've managed to squirrel away a few best sellers … Yeah, I heard. Ruth said confusion is fairly common after surgery because of the anesthesia, but that it should wear off in a few days."

Sunday noon
Ruth to Bella:

"No, Bella, do not bring Bojo. Yes, I know he made her smile, but it's still not appropriate for a nursing home … Okay, rehab center … It's all the same, they just changed the names … It has nothing to do with protecting the innocent … I had actually been planning to go tomorrow, but I can switch to this afternoon if everyone else is going. Has anyone checked with Ginger? … Sometimes people just need a bit of space before they're ready to see the world, that's all … Okay, so we're not the world … Bella stop! I'm going to call and make sure she's up to receiving visitors first … Yes, I'll bring a gift … I don't know, maybe flowers … Yes, I have chocolate … How should I know what Estelle is bringing? I'm hanging up now, Bella. I'll call you back later, after I speak to Ginger."

Day 8
Thursday afternoon
Helen to Bella:

"Do you think Roger missed us yesterday? It was the first Wednesday we missed in almost three years, aside from when they were closed, you know … You're probably right, I bet Ruth did call him. I have to remember to ask her … Yes, I'm sure Howard appreciated you schlepping all those books … But he said he'd already read them all, so just let it go, Bella, and bring them back to the library … Don't you dare send them a bill for the late fees!"

Day 10

Saturday early evening

Ginger to Ruth:

"Hi, Ruth … Yes, I did get all your messages …Yes, and everyone else's. In fact, by the time I got home last night there had to be at least fifty of them on my answering machine, and I was just too tired to answer anyone … Today? … No, my phone is not broken, I unplugged it … He's doing a bit better, thanks for asking. He walked about twenty feet with a walker … No, probably not for another three weeks. At least that's what the physical therapist estimates … Yeah, being alone really sucks. For all my complaining about him, I am surprised by how lonely it is at home and how much I miss him … Thank you for the invitation, but I'm too exhausted to join you tonight. Maybe tomorrow. I'm going to sleep now. Goodbye."

CHAPTER 31 —DARKNESS

Looking around her kitchen, all Ginger could see was the wreckage left over from the previous night's party. Or was that two nights ago? She couldn't remember. Either way, she still hadn't begun to clear the mess ... the one in her head, or the one in her house. Those few dishes that appeared to have been washed had all been randomly stacked in with the dirty ones, making it impossible to differentiate one from the other. A blue-and-white dishcloth hung from the refrigerator handle smeared with crusty streaks of red and brown. It smelled disgusting, even from a distance.

"What the hell did I serve that was red and brown?" Ginger scratched the top of her head, poking her fingers through several knots of stringy red hair as she limped across the room. Grabbing the towel, she lifted it to her nose and gagged. Lingering scents of Worcestershire sauce, guacamole, and bourbon permeated the rag.

"Welcome to my life, folks. Whoop-de-do," she whispered to herself, surveying the damage.

She threw the cloth on the floor and kicked it beneath a mahogany arm chair that had migrated from her living room into the breakfast nook, then stumbled, barely catching herself on the corner of her kitchen counter. Her feet felt … different. She looked down and realized her left foot was bare while her right was firmly wedged in a furry pink bedroom slipper with a one-inch heel.

She made her way down the hall, holding onto the walls for support and turned into the living room. Ashtrays overflowed with cigarette butts and tokes. Wine, beer bottles, and plates of half-eaten congealed food littered the floor and coffee tables. Glassware, ranging from six ounce plastic cups to Waterford champagne goblets, congregated on each surface like mobs of drunken sailors no longer capable of identifying formation by rank.

A wine glass, half-full, stood alone, precariously perched on the edge of her sixty-four inch plasma TV. Her hand seemed to move in slow motion as her fingers closed around the base of the glass, bringing it to eye level. Three of her nails were chipped.

"Manicure. I need a manicure." She sighed. Twirling the stem of the glass, she saw the clear outline of a woman's lips decorating the rim in bright pink lip gloss.

"Ugly color," she muttered, briefly wondering who it belonged to as she brought the glass to her lips, tilted her head back and polished off the sour nectar in two gulps.

The doorbell rang, melodic chimes playing the first few bars of "Für Elyse." Ginger limped toward the sound, her right pink slipper slapping the Italian tiles of the foyer every other step. She flung open the door. Her head buzzed in the bright daylight.

"Bella? What are you doing here?" She shielded her eyes and

thought, *Damn, I need this loud mouth little gnome right now about as much as I need another migraine.*

"Can I come in?"

"Well, it's not really a good time, dear." Ginger pulled her blue satin bathrobe closed.

"I don't care." Bella pushed past her, entered the house, and looked around at the mess. "We've been calling you for a day and a half."

"Why?" Ginger glared at her friend. "It's not Wednesday, is it?"

"No, it's Thursday. You didn't show up at Dante's yesterday, and you haven't been answering your phone. We were worried. So, I decided to come and see for myself if you were still alive."

"Okay, I'm alive. You can leave now."

Bella's face hardened.

Ginger belched. The taste of bile flooded her mouth. *I've got to get her out of here before I throw up,* she thought. She tried to stare down her friend with what she hoped was a menacing scowl. "Whatever you think you're doing here, I don't want it."

"Well, I'm not going," said Bella. Ignoring Ginger's protests and scowls, Bella did a quick lap around the main floor. Then, she took off her coat and rolled up her sleeves. "You'll need help cleaning up this disaster. Then we'll talk. We can begin with the dishes. You collect. I'll wash." Bella headed for the kitchen.

Ginger belched several more times and wandered into the living room. She sat down in her favorite chair beside the hearth, crossed her arms tightly over her chest and rocked back and forth.

The doorbell rang again. More chimes. Ginger didn't move. After two more bars of "Für Elyse," Bella swung open the door to find Ruth, Helen, and Estelle standing on the front stoop. "You guys look just like a bunch of Jehovah's Witnesses waiting at the pearly gates." She chuckled.

Ruth growled.

"Well, you do," Bella insisted, moving out of the way. "You're all so serious."

"Of course we're serious," said Helen. "We were all worried. Is she okay?"

"Not really," answered Bella as she waved the threesome inside.

Estelle spotted Ginger in the living room and went directly to her side. "Do you think you could hold down some tea?" she gently asked.

Ginger looked up, eyes red and dripping, and nodded.

"You just sit there then. I'll get you a cup and be back in a minute."

The ladies gathered in the kitchen area. "Boy, we could really use a social worker about now," Helen remarked.

"Yeah," Ruth agreed, "but the only one we have doesn't seem to be in very good shape."

"Looks like a tornado hit this place."

"That's putting it mildly," Bella said. "I mean, I knew she was having a hard time with Howard being at that rehab place for so long, but I didn't realize she was this low. What do you think we should do?"

"I'm going to try to talk to her for a minute," said Ruth. "Are you guys all right starting the cleanup?"

They nodded.

Estelle perked up. "I'm getting her a cup of tea, and maybe a slice of toast … if I can find the toaster … and the bread. And I'll try to get her washed and dressed when you're done talking."

Without further discussion, the ladies set about their tasks.

Ruth pulled a small hassock in front of Ginger. She dusted off what appeared to be a mixture of ashes, graham cracker crumbs, and dried olives, and sat down.

"So, what's going on?"

Ginger shrugged, eyes cast down.

"How's Howard doing?"

"Getting better." Ginger scoffed. "Walking all over the rehab center. Making progress."

"Progress is good … isn't it?"

"For him, it's been wonderful. For me, not so much."

"Why not?"

Gingers eyes widened with rage.

"Because while he's being taken care of 24/7, he's left me with all the crap work," she snarled. "Bills, repairs, appointments, battles with doctors and insurance companies, computer outages and car breakdowns. Do you know how many years it's been since

I handled any of that stuff?" She looked at Ruth pitifully. "I read all the bills and instructions again and again and again, and I still have no idea what most of them are saying. Howard always insisted on handling it, and now he's gone and left me with it all, and I don't know what to do. It's absolutely overwhelming … and I feel so incompetent, and alone."

"I'm sure he never meant for this to happen, Ginger. Somewhere in your brain you've got to know that." Ruth sighed. "He was ill, and injured, and went through major surgery. Any way you look at it that could not have been easy for him either."

"I know," Ginger moaned. "But every time I go to visit him I find him just kicking back, eating his three square meals a day, making friends and being pampered. He says he's having the time of his life; it's like being on vacation. He's not even sure he wants to come home."

"That's ridiculous. He's got to come home. Doesn't he? I thought it was all set for next week."

"It is. Tuesday morning." Ginger straightened her back and took a deep breath. "Meanwhile, I'm drowning trying to take care of him, and me, and this household." She paused to wipe her nose. "And you want to know the part that upsets me most?"

Ruth shrugged, eyebrows raised.

"It's that when Howard and I first met, I was strong and perfectly capable of handling everything on my own." She wiped away several tears. "The changes in him have been hard enough to deal with, but the changes I see in myself are staggering. I never thought *I* would be so pathetic." Ginger looked into her friend's eyes. Her shoulders sagged. "I'm not doing so well, Ruthie."

"I can tell." Ruth reached out and clasped Ginger's hands. "But I also think you're being way too hard on yourself. Sure, you were once capable of taking care of yourself, and the bills, and the world at large. And you will be again. You're just a tad out of practice now, that's all. Especially in handling all the things that Howard always took care of. You need to cut yourself a little slack. You're doing fine."

Just then, Estelle came by with some tea and toast and a little jar of strawberry jam. She set it down on a snack table near Ginger and quietly left the room without saying a word.

"So," Ruth continued, "did you ever think of asking for help?"

"Of course I did. My neighbor is an accountant, and he said he would help me sort all the household and medical bills and documents and maybe help me figure out Howard's checkbook and payment schedule."

"See," said Ruth, "that's a wonderful start. But I was referring to help as in someone to talk to. A counselor or another social worker."

"Yes. I did that also ... not that it worked out so great. Who the hell do you think tore the place up like this?" She waved her arms around like a conductor, indicating the disastrous mess in the living room.

Ruth shook her head. "I don't understand."

"I called a social worker friend from my old job. A young gal, but very sharp. We worked very well together before I retired. I clearly stated that I was having a huge pity party and could use some help. I said I would supply the dinner and drinks if she would come over to talk and maybe assist me in sorting out some of the emotional chaos I am feeling right now. She was busy, but seemed to be listening attentively as I told her what was going on. In the end, she agreed to come over and asked if she could bring a co-worker. I told her I needed all the help I could get. And they came. Last night." Ginger scratched her head again and plucked a bay leaf from behind her left ear. She looked at it quizzically and tossed it into the hearth. "Or was that two nights ago? I dunno." She looked at Ruth. "What day is today?"

"Thursday."

"Oh," said Ginger. "Well, whenever it was, it turned into a fiasco. She didn't come to help me with my problems. What she did do was invite the entire social services department to my house to have an after work meltdown dinner party."

"What?" shrieked Ruth.

Ginger put a spot of strawberry jam on the toast and took a bite. The dry toast stuck in her throat, and she struggled to swallow it. Ruth handed her the cup of tea and she took a sip, which seemed to help.

"Apparently, the day I called she was preoccupied preparing for a court case, and all she remembered about my entire dire appeal for help was that I was having a party, supplying dinner and drinks, and everyone was welcome." Ginger's face took on a guilty smile.

"And you mean the whole social service department came?"

"Mostly, I think."

"To your house? Just like that?"

"Yep. Party, free food, booze ... Who could resist?"

"How many people showed up?"

"I counted sixteen before the cops came. After that I lost track." Ginger brushed some residual bread crumbs onto the floor, and took another sip of tea. "You know, I had forgotten how young they all are."

"Why in God's name did you let them in?"

"Well, I wasn't going to at first. But then I kept thinking, if Howard is having such a good time at that rehab place, why shouldn't I be having some fun too? So, instead of being mad, I unlocked the front door, cracked open the liquor cabinet, called in an order of deli platters and junk food from our local pub, and ..."

"And?"

"We had a party." Ginger burped.

Ruth blinked.

"And I don't really remember a whole lot after the food arrived."

Ruth shook her head side to side. "I don't know whether to laugh or cry."

"Well, me neither," said Ginger pulling a sprig of lemongrass from between her toes. "I've been doing a lot of both lately."

Helen entered the conversation.

"You really need to sort this all out, dear. And I think you may need professional help to do it right. I know. I've been where you are now, and believe me, it can really make a difference."

Ginger rubbed her forehead and coughed. "You're probably right," she whispered. "The idea has crossed my mind more than once. But there are such long waiting lists to get seen by a therapist, and I never felt connected to any I did manage to speak with." She took another bite of toast. "Do you have anyone in mind?"

"Yes, in fact, I do. There's a group I know of in Portland that specializes in illness and aging and depression. If I get the number for you, will you promise to call for an appointment?"

Ginger nodded.

A second later, they heard Bella shrieking, "I could really use some help back here!" Her words were followed by thunderous crash … and her subsequent whimper: "Too late. Never mind."

The ladies sprinted into the kitchen and found Bella sitting on the floor in a large puddle of soapy water. The completely loaded bottom dishwasher rack was in her lap. A half a dozen pots, pans and innumerable pieces of silverware littered the area around her.

"It's okay," Bella said, looking up with a grin. "None of the glassware broke." At which point two wine goblets toppled off the edge of the sink and shattered, sending shards of crystal everywhere.

After mopping up that mess, the rest of the cleanup continued for several more hours, and was still only partially complete at four o'clock when the ladies decided it was time to leave.

"Howard's definitely coming home Tuesday?" Ruth asked on her way out the door.

"Yes. I'm supposed to pick him up at 9:00 a.m.," Ginger answered. "Assuming he still wants to come home," she added.

"Don't buy into any of that male bravado crap, Ginger," said Bella, putting on her coat. "He's been gone for a month, and I guarantee he wants to come back home so much his teeth hurt."

"I sure hope so," Ginger answered with a crooked smile.

"Which leaves us only four more days to clean up all this mess and get your house ready for human occupancy," Helen added. "So, we better get busy. We'll see you first thing tomorrow morning."

Ginger threw her arms around her friends. "Thank you," she whispered. "I don't know what I'd do without you."

After the ladies left, Ginger limped back into the kitchen and poured herself a cup of strong coffee. She reached into her pocket, pulled out her cell phone, two cloves of garlic and the crumpled paper Helen had given her. Tears streamed down her face as she dialed the number.

"Hello. Yes, my name is Ginger Rosenberg, I'm in trouble and I'd like to make an appointment."

CHAPTER 32 —GARDEN GROWTH

The ladies marched into Pierre's in single file; a solemn procession through the main dining area, around the corner, down the hall past the restrooms, and straight into the banquet room. Not a word was uttered. No laughter, no jokes, no smiles.

Roger saw them out of the corner of his eye but was preoccupied taking breakfast orders from a large party at the front end. He did not notice when Helen broke formation and walked directly behind him. When he spun around, he practically knocked her over.

"Helen," he stuttered, "Are you okay?"

"Yes." Her face was deadpan. "We have a request."

Roger steered her away from the other customers and discreetly handed off the previous table's order sheet to a passing waitress. "What is it?" he asked, concerned.

"We want to be left alone."

Roger cocked his head to the side. "I don't understand. You don't want breakfast?

"Of course we do. That's why we come in here. But we want

you to take our orders quickly, serve us, and then leave the room and not come back in again until we call you."

Bella ambled up behind the two of them. "You know, it's time you got a real door on that room. Those stupid red-and-gold drapes do not afford any privacy."

"I'm sorry," said Roger, "but that's what the owner wants."

"Well, please ask him if he would spring for a door one of these days. Tell him it would be *very* appreciated," said Helen.

"I'll tell him," said Roger, "but it was hard enough getting him to agree to expand the banquet room and paint it yellow. I don't think he's going to budge on anything else."

Bella ogled the order pad and pen in Roger's shirt pocket. "Can I borrow your pen?" she asked.

Roger handed Bella his pen.

"Okay, what's his name?"

"Whose name?" asked Roger, tugging at his left earlobe.

"The new owner, of course," answered Bella. "I'm going to write him a letter."

Roger laughed.

"Well, give it to me," Bella insisted.

"His name is Mr. Bruce Salmonsmith."

"Salmon what?" asked Bella.

"Salmonsmith."

"Not Tuna Fish?"

Bella laughed as she wrote *Salmonsmith* on the back of her left hand in black ink. "And what's a good address for Mr. Cod

Cakes?"

Roger's face turned red. "I guess you can write to him at this address."

"Okay." Bella returned Roger's pen, spun around, and headed back toward the banquet room.

"Can I ask what this is all about?"

"No," Helen said, toddling after Bella. "We'll be ready to order in just a few minutes."

By the time she joined her friends in the back room, the red-and-gold paneled drapes had already been drawn closed.

Hearty laughter from the front counter caught Roger's attention. He walked over to Ralph, one of the breakfast regulars, and shrugged.

"The old broads giving you a hard time again this morning?" Ralph asked, grinning from ear to ear.

"Yep. God only knows what they're up to this time." Roger sighed. "It's just that they're so serious and quiet. They're never quiet. Not sure what to make of it."

"They never even popped their heads into the kitchen to say good morning to me, and they always do that," added Desmond, joining the conversation.

"Wish I could help." Ralph chuckled. "But since you moved them into that back room, I don't get to see them anymore. Eavesdropping on their conversations was always the highlight of my day." He slapped ten dollars on the counter to cover his bill. "I miss the old broads," he said as he sauntered out of the café.

Roger took five glasses of ice water into the back room. He studied the old ladies, trying to glean any hint of what they were up to, but was met with five blank stares. He placed one glass of water in front of each lady and stood back. "Are you ready to order now?" he asked.

"Yes, thank you. I'll go first," said Ruth.

The ladies ordered in record time and sat back to wait. "Please tell Desmond to hurry up today," said Estelle. "We've got business to attend to, and we can't get started until all the breakfasts have been delivered and we can have some privacy."

"I'll let him know. I'm sure he'll do his best. Is there anything else I can get for you?"

The ladies declined.

Roger returned a few minutes later with their coffee and tea. He put two baskets of fresh rolls on the table and then started doling out the breakfast orders.

When he set the last order down, he asked one final time, "Anything else?"

"Yes," Ginger said. "Your promise that you won't come in here unless we say it's okay."

"And even then, be sure to knock on the curtain first," added Estelle.

As soon as Roger left, Ginger jumped up and pinched both panels of drapes together while Bella fastened them with a half dozen antique wooden clothespins she had brought with her. The ladies were all slightly flushed as they prepared to get down to business.

Fifteen minutes passed before Desmond poked his head out of the kitchen, gesturing for Roger to come closer.

"What?" Roger asked.

"They've begun to giggle," said Desmond.

"You can hear them?"

"Yes. They opened one of their windows, which is only a few feet away from the kitchen window where I'm preparing the salads."

"Can you hear what they're saying?"

"Nope," said Desmond. "But they're not crying, that's for sure."

Roger took a deep breath. "Well, I'll settle for that. I thought for sure one of them was dying, or something. I've just never seen them so grim."

Desmond returned to the kitchen, and Roger went back to his other customers. Another fifteen minutes passed before Desmond called to Roger again.

"Now what?" Roger asked.

"Well, you don't have to worry about them being quiet any longer. They're getting louder by the minute."

"Any tears?"

"Are you kidding? I'm surprised you haven't heard them. They're laughing their heads off."

"Okay," said Roger, relieved. "Good to know."

"Well, there's something else you should know." Desmond's lips parted into a huge grin, flashing a full set of pearly-white teeth. His eyes beamed with laughter.

Roger cocked his head to the side. "All right. What?"

"There's more than laughter drifting through my window at this moment, man. Your old ladies are back there in the banquet room smokin' weed."

Roger's jaw dropped. So did the half-full pitcher of orange juice he had been carrying. "You're joking, right?"

"No, man, I am not," said Desmond, picking up large chunks of broken glass and grabbing the mop. "Your angels are flying high this morning," he laughed. "Doin' cartwheels in the sky!"

"I don't believe you! They can't. I mean, they wouldn't," Roger exclaimed. "They're old!"

"Well, they can, and they will, and they are," said Desmond, laughing. "Come over here by the window and take a whiff for yourself, if you don't believe me."

Roger went to the window and inhaled. "Holy crap!" He shook his head side to side. "So, that's what this morning's antics were all about? Privacy, so they could get stoned?"

Desmond continued to smirk as he finished with the mop, flipped a half a dozen pancakes, and scrambled a batch of eggs. "I didn't know old ladies in this country did that sort of thing. Now, back in my country ..."

"No, no, no, no, no!" Roger suddenly shouted. "I just remembered, they can't be doing that today! Not now! The boss is on his way over here to meet them all."

Desmond's face blanched. "Bruce is coming here during the breakfast rush? Why? He never shows up before four."

"He's coming early because I called and begged him to come, not twenty minutes ago." Roger pounded his fists against his forehead. "Helen pleaded with me for a door to the banquet room this morning, and she looked so sad ... and Bella was threatening to write him a letter. Oh, crap. I thought if he met them, they could convince the tight-ass bastard to get a door to that back room, and everyone would be happy."

"Oh, shit," said Desmond, plating several dishes of scrambled eggs in quick succession and topping them with toast, bacon and ripe raspberries. "Then you'd better get in there and sober them up in a hurry!" Desmond ordered.

"You know, the son of a bitch might just shut this whole damn place down if he finds any weed back there," said Roger.

Desmond nodded, wide-eyed. "Better take the big fan from the storage room with you. Maybe you can blow some smoke outside."

"What about my tables?" Roger asked, emptying a dust pan of broken glass into the trash bin.

"Don't worry about them. If Bruce is on his way, we've got bigger problems. I'll call Ilsa and see if she can cover for you. She lives around the corner and is always looking for extra shifts. Just go!"

Roger tossed his order pad to Desmond, wrestled the fan out

of the storage closet and headed for the banquet room. He pushed through the curtains, sending half a dozen clothespins leaping like grasshoppers in all directions.

The first thing he saw through a thick blanket of smoke was Estelle, perched on top of one of the tables, twirling an iridescent pink feathered boa and swaying to music that seemed to be coming from Helen's iPhone. He gasped, waving his arm back and forth to clear the fumes. He thought the women might freak out at being discovered. Instead, Ginger grabbed his hand and began dancing around him while all the other ladies continued laughing and clapping in time to the music.

"Stop it!" he shouted, pulling away.

"Here, take a puff of this," said Bella, offering him a small glass pipe. "It'll make you feel a lot better," she giggled.

Roger grabbed the pipe and dunked it in the closest glass of water, then ran toward the windows and threw them both wide open. He plugged in the fan and aimed it at the ladies, which only made them laugh harder.

"Ruth," he called, "You've always been the sensible one. Can you please help me with this group? My boss is on his way over here to meet you all, and I will probably get fired if he finds you like this."

Ruth stared back at him, her eyes glazed. "You know, I've always loved the color purple," she said, stroking her purple tote as if it were a kitten. "Even when I was a little girl."

"Ruth, snap out of it. I need you, now!" said Roger, gently

shaking her shoulders.

Ruth took his hand and whispered, "If you buy me a dog, I promise to name it Purple, Roger."

"Purple Roger," Helen mimicked. "I like that. Purple Roger, Purple Roger, Purple Roger." She kept repeating *Purple Roger* while bobbing her head up and down to the beat of the current song.

The music on Helen's iPhone suddenly changed from calypso, to a ballad by R. Kelly called *'I Believe I Can Fly'*. Estelle seemed to know all the words and began singing along in some kind of misguided harmony. Then she stepped closer to the edge of the table, sang one more chorus of *'I Believe I Can Fly'*, and began flapping her arms.

"No!" Roger roared.

Estelle jumped. Roger lunged, and somehow managed to catch her, mostly. She was still smiling a few seconds later, after they tumbled onto the floor, so he figured she wasn't hurt. He stood up and helped her into a chair, ignoring the pain in his own ankle.

"Jesus! What the hell have you guys been smoking?" he asked, staring at the group.

The red-and-gold panels parted, and Desmond stuck his head through. "Oh boy! They're in even worse shape than I thought. What can I do to help?" he asked.

"Shoot me," Roger answered.

"Maybe some black coffee?"

"I'll try anything."

"How much time you think we've got before Bruce gets here?"

Roger looked at his watch. "If he left his office right after I called, maybe a half hour, at most."

Ginger came up from behind and latched onto Roger's left shoulder. "Remember when you asked if I needed anything?" she murmured seductively.

"Yes," said Roger, gently peeling her hands off his arm.

"Well, I need a bucket."

Roger stepped back a bit. "Why do you need a bucket?"

"Because," she burped, "I'm going to throw up."

"Oh …" Roger said, inhaling sharply. He spun Ginger toward the ladies' room. "There's a big waste bin in there, and a toilet. Try the toilet first."

Ginger nodded as he opened the bathroom door and shoved her inside.

Desmond appeared with half a dozen mugs and two carafes of coffee. "Well, the air is almost transparent now," he joked. "Good job." He took a can of lemon-scented room deodorizer from his back pocket and sprayed down the whole room.

Ginger returned to the group looking rather pale.

Roger turned off the music, got the ladies seated around the tables, and put a steaming cup of coffee in front of each of them. "Were you able to reach Ilsa?" he asked Desmond.

"Yep. She's here already. Your tables are covered."

Little by little the ladies stopped giggling. They stayed in the seats that Roger assigned, hands clasped in front like a bunch of schoolgirls, and smiled at him adoringly.

Feeling like a teacher in front of a group of misbehaving third graders, he asked again, "Okay, what in God's name have you ladies been smoking?"

Ginger shrugged. Helen blinked. Bella put her head down on the table and began to snore. Ruth continued to stroke her purple tote.

"Estelle?" asked Roger.

Estelle smiled timidly.

"Do you know what you were smoking?"

"The stuff in this little brown bag," she whispered.

"What little brown bag?" Roger asked.

Estelle reached into the pocket of her floppy blue cardigan and pulled out a small crinkled brown bag. She handed it to Roger.

Roger opened the bag, sniffed the contents, coughed and rolled his eyes. "Where the hell did you get this crap?"

"My grandson."

"Your grandson sold you this?"

"Of course not! He's a good boy. He would never charge me for anything. I found it in the guest room after his last visit."

Desmond burst out laughing as he lifted the bag from Roger and stuck it in his back pocket, alongside the room freshener. "I think I'll go back into the kitchen now," he said, disappearing behind the red-and-gold drapes.

Estelle looked up, wide-eyed. "Can I ask you a question?"

"Sure," Roger answered more gently.

"Where's my lottery ticket? I get one every week. Did you forget?"

Roger sighed. "I'm sorry, Estelle, but we're not selling lottery tickets anymore."

Estelle's lower lip began to tremble, and she started to cry. "Why?" she asked, tears running down her cheeks.

"Well, Bruce, that is, Mr. Salmonsmith, is a rather straight-laced dude. He doesn't believe in gambling ... in any form. When he found out we were selling lottery tickets, he had a fit. So, we don't sell them anymore."

"But what am I going to do?" Estelle cried. "I need them so that we can all become millionaires."

Roger rolled his eyes and handed Estelle a tissue. "Please don't cry. There's a place just two doors down that sells them," he offered.

"The Coconut Bar and Grill?"

"Yes," said Roger. "Dumb name, but a nice place. They sell lots of lottery tickets. I'm sure you can get one there."

"Ginger won't let us go in that place anymore because she had a fight with Carl in the bathtub," Estelle whimpered, "but maybe I can sneak in before we all gather here and she won't notice."

"I'm sitting right next to you, Estelle. I can hear you," Ginger said loudly.

"Oh," murmured Estelle.

"And it's okay with me if you want to go into that place. I'll just wait outside. But why you feel the need to buy all those damn tickets is beyond me." She scowled. "It's a total waste of money."

Ruth's eyes seemed a bit more focused. "Do you have any aspirin?" she asked, looking up at Roger.

"Sure. I'll get you some." He disappeared for a few minutes. When he returned, he handed Ruth a bottle of Advil. "How are you feeling?"

"I'm not sure yet," she said. "This stuff had a lot more kick than the pot I'm used to." She rubbed her temples and swallowed two tablets.

Desmond stuck his head through the curtain again. "You all smoke weed?"

"Well," Ruth sighed, "not anymore. But I used to. Everyone did back in the sixties."

"You would have also, if you had been around," added Helen.

"The sixties?" Desmond chuckled. "That was a half century ago, ma'am. Times have changed. So has weed."

"Actually, me and Jake used to grow our own stuff in a window box in our apartment in Greenwich Village," Ginger reflected.

"The things I never knew about you!" said Helen.

"Jake insisted we be organic, even back then. No pesticides or herbicides. But, when the leaves all became infested with aphids, we couldn't use it anymore, so Jake just dumped the whole batch down the building's main garbage chute. I think everyone in the entire neighborhood got high the day the landlord fired up our incinerator." She giggled. "But that's another story. After the first fiasco of growing our own failed, we went back to buying … whatever."

Estelle snuggled next to Ruth. "Who's Jake again? I forgot."

"Jake in the bathtub, in Atlantic City," Ruth whispered.

"I thought Carl was in the bathtub," said Estelle.

"No. Carl is the waiter from the Coconut Bar and Grill. Jake in the bathtub was Ginger's first husband."

"Oh. So, who's Howard?"

Ruth sighed. "I'll tell you all about it later, dear."

Ginger began rubbing a new hive blossoming on her neck. "Estelle thought her grandson's marijuana was medicinal, for his toothache. Since there was some left-over, we thought it would be fun to try again," she said, reaching for her tube of cortisone.

"Well, this mix is a lot stronger than any medicinal kind of weed you can buy in a reputable place," Desmond stated. "And from the look of you ladies, it was laced with something you should not be fooling around with. You ladies have got to be more careful of things like this. They can kill you," he scolded.

Bella snorted so loudly that she woke herself up. She propped her chin on her hands and partially opened her eyes. "Yeah, I kinda got that impression," she mumbled, then closed her eyes and put her head down again.

"Are you all going to get in trouble because of us?" asked

Ruth.

"I'm not sure," Roger answered without looking up.

Ilsa pushed aside the drapes and stepped into the room. "Telephone for you, Roger. It's the boss."

Roger took a deep breath and grimaced. "Okay," he said, leaving the room, "I'll be back in a few minutes … I hope."

"Hello, Mr. Salmonsmith, this is Roger. What? … Are you okay? … The front bumper *and* the passenger door? Where are they towing it? … Yeah, that's a good place. Do you need a lift? … Well, call if you need anything … Yes, sir, I'm sure the ladies will be disappointed … Yes, sir, I will explain the situation and send your apologies … Of course they'll understand. Yes, we'll see you tomorrow."

Roger hung up the phone and leaned back against the wall. "Yes!" he shouted, pumping the air with both fists. Desmond and Ilsa sighed with relief.

The ladies stayed in the banquet room of Pierre's until almost one o'clock before slowly filtering out to the parking lot.

"I thought Roger was going to keep us in there forever," said Helen.

Ruth hoisted the straps of her purple tote over her shoulder. "He just wanted to make sure we were safe to drive, dear."

"I know," Helen whined. "It just seems that we were having breakfast so long that it turned into lunch and dinner."

"Maybe that's why I'm hungry again," added Estelle.

Ginger applied a third layer of cortisone cream to her hive. "I think from now on if we want to try any drugs we better buy them," she said. "That way we'd at least know what we were getting."

"One would hope so," Ruth added.

"Well, I personally am done for a while," answered Estelle. "I feel like my brain has been nuked in the microwave."

Bella began to laugh. "I was just thinking, wouldn't it be funny if tomorrow's headlines read 'Five Old Ladies Overdose in Local Restaurant.' "

The ladies stared at her.

"You are so weird," said Helen.

"I know," giggled Bella.

"You know, this Mr. Salomon-cod seems like a real jerk," said Ginger.

Helen agreed. "I got the distinct feeling that all was not well in the Emerald City."

"What city?" asked Bella.

"The Emerald City." Helen gave an exasperated huff. "Oh, never mind. I meant all's not well at Pierre's."

Ginger put away her tube of cortisone cream and checked the size of her hive in the side mirror of a nearby Subaru. "I think you're right," she said. "Now that you mention it, the restaurant is not nearly as crowded as it used to be."

"Well, the food is still good, thanks to Desmond," Bella commented, "but the décor stinks, and so does the name. Pierre's? Really?"

"Do you think the place is in trouble?" asked Estelle.

"Could be," said Ruth. "They do seem to have cut back on the size of the food portions, and the wait staff."

"And the lottery tickets," added Estelle.

"And I've noticed they don't sell wine anymore either," said Ginger.

Bella chuckled. "You would notice that."

Estelle suddenly broke from the group.

"Estelle? Where are you going?" Ruth called out.

"Thank you for reminding me! I'm off to buy my lottery ticket at the Coconut Bar and Grill, along with a whisky chaser, I think," she said over her shoulder. "See you all next week!"

And a moment later she was gone.

CHAPTER 33 —YAKS

"This onion roll is as hard as a rock," Ruth said, pounding the small biscuit on the table. A chunk broke off, bounced once, and landed in Estelle's water glass.

"I think it's Josie's birthday today. Has anyone heard from her this week?" asked Estelle, trying to spoon the chunk from her drink.

Ginger was absentmindedly filing her jagged left thumbnail. "She just took delivery of eleven yaks. Can you even imagine doing something like that?" She looked up momentarily, then continued filing her nail.

"Josie's got eleven yaks?" Estelle put down her spoon.

"What the hell is she doing with eleven yaks?" asked Bella, stuffing a glob of scrambled eggs in her mouth and grimacing. "Humph," she muttered. She wiped her lips with a red cloth napkin. "These eggs are very greasy. And salty."

Helen put down her large text crossword puzzle. "Who's got eleven yaks?"

"Jocinda," answered Ginger, carefully examining her other

nails.

Ruth poured three packets of sugar into her coffee. "Who's Jocinda?"

Helen scrunched her face. "And since when do you take sugar in your coffee?"

"Since today, I guess. The coffee is very bitter this morning," said Ruth.

"What's a yak?" asked Estelle, as she resumed fishing little breadcrumbs from her drink.

"They're like cows, only a lot uglier," Ginger answered. She put away her nail file and picked up her iPhone. "Here, I'll show you a picture of one." Ginger looked up *yak* on Google and showed the picture to Estelle, who handed the phone around to all the other ladies.

"What's all that stringy stuff hanging down from their sides?" asked Helen.

"And who is Jocinda?" Ruth asked again, pushing a clump of burnt home fries to the edge of her plate.

Ginger expanded the picture and scrunched her nose. "It's hair, I think. Or fur. Good for making scarves, according to Google." She tucked her phone back into her purse.

"They kinda remind me of what my great aunt Lillian looked like after she got caught in a rainstorm last summer," said Bella.

"Well, I don't understand why she needed eleven of them," said Helen. "Couldn't you make a scarf with just one?"

Estelle's eyebrows knit together. "In my building, they won't even allow dogs."

Ginger looked at Estelle. "Excuse me, but were you talking about Josie?"

Estelle nodded.

"Geez, I haven't heard from Josie in ages. At least not since she and Arthur moved to Utah." Ginger spit a wad of pink bubblegum into a tissue and reached for the last packet of orange marmalade before Estelle grabbed it.

"What?" Bella screeched, "Josie moved to Utah? When the hell did that happen?"

"About a month ago. I'm sure I told you all." Ginger stared blankly at her friends. "Didn't I?"

"No!" said Ruth sharply.

"Sorry." Ginger shrugged. "My bad."

"Why did they move to Utah?" asked Estelle. "I heard that's an awful place to live."

"I'm not sure. I received some sort of generic letter from them. It was about the time Howard was in that rehab place, so I guess I didn't really pay much attention to it."

"Well, what *do* you remember?" asked Helen, tossing her crossword puzzle to the side.

"Let's see," said Ginger. She twirled the ends of several long strands of hair. "Apparently, they became even closer to their cruising buddies, the Steinbergs and their golfing buddies."

"Bert and Ernie," Bella interrupted.

"Who?" asked Estelle.

"Albert and Ernestine Hornblower," Helen whispered.

"Yes," said Ginger, "and the three couples packed up and moved to some pricey vacation area in Utah. That's about all I remember."

"And they never even let the rest of us know? After all these years?" Ruth questioned.

"Apparently not," said Bella.

Estelle began drawing sad faces on her napkin with a brown eyeliner pencil. "Well, I hope they're happy," she whispered quietly. "Though I do think it would have been nice if she had told us."

"The truth is, I never really liked her anyway," said Bella.

"Hmm. Now that you mention it, neither did I," added Ginger. "I always thought she was kind of stuck up around us, on the few occasions when she did bother to show up."

"She might have been stuck up, but she did have a lot of beautiful jewelry," added Helen.

There was silence for a few minutes before the conversation resumed.

"Okay, so how did she manage to get eleven yaks shipped to Utah? Or did she just buy them there?" Helen asked, putting a lump of butter on a slice of burnt toast.

"It wasn't Josie who had the yaks," answered Ginger sharply. "It was Jocinda."

Ruth slammed down the salt shaker. "For the last time, who is Jocinda?" she yelled. "And why are we even talking about her?"

Helen scrunched her face again. "I personally don't care who Jocinda is. What I want to know is how she got eleven yaks into her condo."

"They must have a very large freight elevator," answered Estelle, nodding her head.

Ginger huffed loudly. "What is wrong with all of you today?" She stared at her friends. "Jocinda is my adopted daughter. She was on my mind this morning, and I got Josie and Jocinda mixed up for a minute, so shoot me! Jocinda and her husband own a farm in upstate Maine, and they just got eleven yaks to add to their menagerie … end of story. Geez Louise."

She reached into her purse for a small bottle of purple nail polish and began applying a thin coat to her thumbnail. "And what all this has to do with Josie, I have no idea," she added, then she took a bite of her pancake and spit it out in her napkin. "Uck! This tastes awful!"

Estelle stared at Ginger. "I didn't know you had an adopted daughter."

A slow smile brightened Ginger's face.

"Well, she's not officially adopted. Just in my heart. She is one of my daughter's old college roommates. We've always stayed in touch."

Just then, Roger swung by. "Everything all right?" he asked.

"Not really," Ruth answered quietly.

"The food really stinks this morning," barked Bella. "Is Desmond hungover or something?"

Roger lowered his head. His face was drawn and fatigued. "Desmond doesn't work here anymore," he stuttered after a long pause.

The ladies sat in stunned silence for what seemed like an eternity.

"What happened?" Ruth whispered at last.

"He was fired."

The ladies stared at him.

"Why?" asked Estelle. "He was lovely. And his food was always delicious."

"Yeah," said Bella shoving her plate to the side. "Not like this garbage."

"Was it because of us smoking pot last month?" asked Estelle.

"No, not at all," he assured them. "Thank God the boss never found out about that or he probably would have fired us all."

"Then why?" asked Helen.

"Well," Roger sighed, "the restaurant hasn't really been doing so great since Mr. Salmonsmith took over, and he needed to cut costs. Unfortunately, Desmond was one of those costs."

"So, who's doing the cooking?" asked Helen.

"His name is Julien. He's Mr. Salmonsmith's eighteen-year-old nephew."

"Has he ever taken any cooking lessons?" Bella asked.

Roger shook his head side-to-side.

"Oh, good grief!" said Helen. No wonder everything tastes awful."

"And Mr. Cod Cakes thinks business will improve if he poisons us all?" asked Bella.

Ruth put her half-eaten plate of food on top of Bella's discarded dish and leaned back in her chair. "When did this all happen?" she asked Roger.

"Last Friday, at the end of his shift," Roger answered quietly. "The boss called him into the office, handed him a pink slip along with his check for the week, and had the security guard walk him right out of the building."

"Security guard?" squealed Ginger. "Since when do you have a security guard around here?"

"Since Friday." Roger shifted his weight nervously from one foot to the other. "I think he was hired especially for that day, because one janitor and two of our waitresses were also let go in the same way. Pink slip, check, and escorted out the door."

"Ilsa?" Ruth asked.

"Gone."

"That is so incredibly sad, and mean. Why do people do things like that?" said Helen, gritting her teeth.

"What gets me is that he didn't even let any of them go back into the staff room and pack up their own belongings. After they were gone, the rest of the staff had to box up all their stuff and put it at the back entrance for them to collect later."

"Escorted out?" Bella snapped. "Why? Because Mr. Bigshot was afraid someone might steal a jar of his precious mayonnaise?"

"I assume Desmond doesn't have any other job lined up," Ruth asked Roger.

"Nope. It was a total surprise, so nothing yet." He shuffled back and forth. "Can I get you ladies anything else?"

"No," said Ruth. "I don't think so."

"Just our checks, please," added Helen.

Roger walked out of the small banquet room, leaving the silent band of unhappy ladies behind.

"I just don't understand this world anymore," said Ruth, scratching the top of her head. "And I seem to be saying that more and more often," she added, quietly.

Helen bit down on her lower lip. "The workplace has gotten very mean in recent years. It wasn't always like this. Years ago, when I first started out, people treated each other with dignity and respect."

"Some places were better than others, but now it seems they are all turning nasty," said Ruth. "I remember taking all of my personal belongings home from the office the day *before* I gave notice. I learned that the hard way when some of my co-workers were escorted out the door the moment they quit. And that was fifteen years ago. In a hospital … a supposed gentle place of healing and respite."

Bella burped. She pulled a tissue from her sleeve, blew her nose, and threw the used tissue in the middle of the table. No one pushed it aside. "You know," she said, burping again, "my friend worked for an orthopedic surgeon for twenty-three years as his office manager. He used to tell her that she was part of his family, and she really felt as though she was. Well, the doctor had a nasty little son who was spoiled rotten. My friend watched the kid grow up, go to medical school, and eventually he joined his father's practice." Bella reached for another tissue and wiped her nose. "And the first thing he did," she continued, "was to fire my friend."

"Why?" asked the ladies in unison.

"The new doctor-brat told his dad that the office staff was too old and he needed younger people."

"And the father listened to him?" ask Estelle.

"Yep," Bella sighed.

Ruth looked down at the cracked floor tile under her left foot. "I know what that feels like," she whispered.

"Excuse me," said Roger, somberly walking into the banquet room with the ladies' checks. He handed all the individual checks to Helen. "You may want to look these over more carefully than usual today," he said as he left the room. Helen separated the checks and scanned each one as if she was checking for forgeries.

"What's up?" asked Bella.

"The price," answered Helen. "I'd say about 10 percent."

"For this crap?" Bella snapped.

Helen distributed the checks to her friends.

"Guess it's time to start looking around for a new place again," Ruth murmured.

"I guess so," said Helen. "Quite a day of losses. Desmond, Ilsa …"

"And Josie," added Ginger.

Estelle began frantically rummaging through her purse.

"Oh no!" she squealed. "I changed pocketbooks this morning, and I think I forgot to put my wallet in this new bag! I'm destitute!" she wailed.

"I guess you'll just have to stay behind and wash all the dishes after we go home," said Bella, grinning impishly.

"But I didn't bring my rubber gloves!" cried Estelle.

Ruth gave Bella a nasty glance. "Don't worry, honey. I'll cover it," she said, pulling out her credit card.

Bella laughed. "Well, Estelle, you seem to have lucked out this time, but remember, Ruth knows where you live and can track you down if you don't pay her back with interest by next week."

"Really?" whimpered Estelle.

"Of course not!" Ruth, Helen, and Ginger yelled. The next time Bella opened her mouth to say something Ruth kicked her under the table. Bella closed her mouth and swallowed her next comment.

"But my lottery ticket. I can't buy one this week without a full dollar and all I can find at the bottom of this purse is forty-six cents in change."

"Well, how about if this week we all chip in and buy a few of those mega tickets together," said Ginger.

"But where?" Estelle asked.

"Well, the only nearby place I know of is the Coconut Bar and Grill."

"Would you really do that?" Estelle asked.

"Sure, why not," answered Helen. "But just this once … in memory of Desmond. Even though I still think it is a total waste of money."

"Can you imagine us as five millionaires?" laughed Ginger.

"There's an expression for that," said Bella, tossing another used tissue onto the table.

"From your mouth to God's ear," Helen interrupted.

"Yeah. That's the one. From your mouth to God's ear," Bella repeated, chuckling.

It was almost eleven thirty when the ladies paid their bills and waved goodbye to Roger. A cool breeze floated over the group as they made their way out to the street.

Estelle leaned over to Ruth. "I think I have to go back inside again," she said quietly.

"Why? Did you forget something?"

"No," she whispered. "I have to go to the bathroom again. Would you wait for me?"

"Of course, dear," said Ruth.

A few minutes later Estelle popped out of the front door, and the two of them rushed to catch up with the other ladies down the block.

"I was wondering," Estelle puffed, "do you think we should include Josie in the winnings of the lottery tickets from now on?"

"No, dear," said Ruth. "She's moved on. I think it's time for us to let her go."

Estelle pouted.

Ruth put her arm around Estelle's shoulders. "Just remember, this was her choice, not ours, so there's no need for you to feel bad about it."

Estelle nodded. "You're probably right, Ruthie," she said, sadly. "I guess it's just the five of us from now on." Still tightly clutching her forty-six cents, she took a deep breath and hobbled forward.

Ruth and Estelle caught up to the others at the Coconut Bar and Grill just in time to join the group in the purchase of ten brightly colored lottery tickets.

CHAPTER 34—FOR SALE

Friday: 11:00 a.m.

Helen to Ruth:

"Ruth! Did you hear? Dante's, I mean Pierre's, is up for sale! ... I just happened to be driving by the place on my way to get paper towels and deodorant from Target. You wouldn't believe the fantastic sales they have this week, *and* I also had an additional 30 percent coupon from the local paper for their organic denture cream ... Well, not now, but one never knows how long teeth are going to last ... Oh yes, about Dante's ... Well, there was this huge *For Sale* sign on the lawn right in front of the building ... I tried to get the phone number, but I couldn't read the small print. Some guy in a giant black truck kept honking his horn every time I stopped long enough for my eyes to focus ... I've already told you, I'm going for an eye exam soon ... You're going past Dante's tomorrow? ... Great! Let me know what you find out."

Friday: 11:10 a.m.

Helen to Bella:

"Bella, guess what! I passed by Dante's this morning, and the place has closed down and is up for sale again … What do you mean it's still open? How do you know? … You and Ginger? … Now? … Without the rest of us? … Well, goody for you two … No, I'm not mad … So, is the food any better on Fridays? ... Well, don't forget to copy down the phone number from the sign outside … Of course it's important. Ruth wants to know … We have to check out who Mr. Cod Cakes is selling to."

Saturday: 2:30 p.m.
Estelle to Ruth:

"But Bella said it was closing at the end of the week … I'm confused, Ruth, is the end of the week this Friday, or the next one? … Oh, you're right, this Friday was yesterday … Good, that means we can still go at our regular time this coming Wednesday … I just really want to say goodbye to Roger … I was also wondering if I could hitch a ride with you … No, I'm fine. David has a doctor's appointment, and I said he could take the car … Yes, twice this month, but only fender benders … Me too … Oh well, I sure hope somebody nice buys the place."

Sunday: 11:00 a.m.
Ginger to Bella:

"My friend, Doris, is a real estate broker who deals in commercial properties, and she said Pierre's is selling for $875,000 … Really? … Well, I personally thought a fine establishment like that would go for a lot more … It is *not* a dump! … Okay, so it's not exactly prime property either … I know the inside décor is hideous, but that should be a quick fix, shouldn't it? ... Why are you being so negative, Bella? ... I'm just saying that if we all chipped in ... No, I don't know anything about your medical expenses ... I had a lot also ... Insurance? Ha! ... I'm just trying to be creative to see if there is any way we can save Dante's, that's all ... No, the only millionaires I know don't talk to me either ... Okay, maybe when we get together Wednesday, we can come up with a plan."

Monday: 11:30 a.m.

Bella to Helen:

"Calm down, Helen ... Yes, I heard all about Ginger's plan ... Well, what did you expect from a bleeding-heart, ditsy liberal? ... Of course I like her—she's just an idiot ... None of us have that kind of loot to throw around, except maybe Estelle ... Well, I was thinking of all those $100 bills we found in-between her dishes last fall. And she never did tell us how much she found stuffed inside her mattress, did she? ... Medicare fraud? I hadn't thought of that ... Not Estelle; maybe David, though ... I'd love to, but I'm babysitting Bojo all afternoon. Oh, crap! He must've heard your voice, he just woke up from his nap screaming ... Speaker phone, of course ... Well, the kid obviously still hates you ... Listen, I gotta go. See you Wednesday."

Monday: 4:15 p.m.

Ruth to Ginger:

"I know you didn't mean to get everyone upset, Ginger, but personal finances are, well, personal. None of us have oodles of money, or experience in this area … Honestly, that is *so not* realistic … Well, what *do* you know about running a restaurant? … I'm sorry, but eating in them all your life does *not* count … No, neither does watching Chef Irvine on *Restaurant Impossible* … Because … Whatever … Okay, I'll think about it … I'm sure Roger will tell us what's happening, assuming he's still there … Well, it is a possibility … Okay, bye."

Tuesday: 8:45 p.m.

Ruth to Estelle:

"Hi, Estelle. I heard your message on my answering machine last night, but it was too late to call you back. What's on your mind? … Oh, so you heard about Ginger's plan to buy the restaurant? … Well, please don't give it another thought. It's a totally ridiculous idea … You agree with her? … Estelle, owning a restaurant is not like taking in one of your rescue Chihuahuas … What do you mean, angels? Like in the theater when you support the cause? … Estelle, I'm sorry, dear, but I just don't have the time for this right now, or the money, for that matter … Okay, I'll think about it … You have a good day also, and I'll pick you up at 8:30 tomorrow morning."

CHAPTER 35 —ANGELS

The following Wednesday morning the ladies gathered in the cafe's parking lot for the last time. There was a lot of sniffling and hand-wringing as they walked quietly toward the entrance of Pierre's. Ginger and Estelle sighed repeatedly, fighting back tears. Ruth opened the front door, and the group squished into the small outer vestibule.

"It still looks like Campbell's tomato and rice soup in here, doesn't it?" Helen said, rubbing her hand along the lumpy red walls.

Bella opened the inner door, allowing the ladies to gradually filter through to the main dining room, where they stood silently looking around, taking in the garish red, and brown, and gold walls. Barely a half dozen customers were present.

"I can't believe I'm going to miss this ugly place," said Bella.

"Well, I'm still optimistic," Ginger stated. "Something good is going to come of all this, you'll see. It has to."

The ladies wound their way through the dining room, around the corner, down the hall, past the restrooms, and filed into their little banquet room. Bella grabbed the first plush chair she saw and dragged it to the far corner under the window. "We obviously won't need a seat for Josie anymore," she stated, as the rest of the group settled in.

Roger entered, a semi-sweet expression etched on his face. "Good morning, ladies. How're you all doing today?"

"Oh," Ruth sighed with relief. "It is so good to see you!"

Ginger ran up to him and swung her arms around his neck. Tears streamed down her face. "We were all so worried that you would be gone, and we would never get the chance to say goodbye."

Estelle clapped her hands joyously and then dipped into the neckline of her chartreuse sweater with the hot-pink embroidered flamingos, pulled a lacy handkerchief from the right side of her bosom, and wiped her eyes. "We weren't sure you'd still be here," she stammered.

"Aw, come on, ladies, it's not as bad as all that!" said Roger, gently peeling Ginger off his neck. "Nobody died."

"But you're closing," whimpered Estelle.

"Yes—but not 'til Friday." Roger grinned at them. "That's a world away. Who knows what can happen until then. So … who wants breakfast?"

"Ugh," groaned Bella. "If that little twerp, Julien, is still in the kitchen, I'll pass. He should be arrested for what he does to an egg."

"I'll pass, too," said Ruth. "Just a cup of coffee, please."

"Who's got the short-term memory loss now?" whined Helen, staring at Ruth. "Did you already forget what Julien did to your coffee?" Helen fidgeted with her napkin. "You told me you had the runs for hours after your breakfast last week, and you barely had anything, except the coffee."

"Oh, you're right," said Ruth. "Change my order to a cup of boiling water and a tea bag, please. Hopefully, Julien won't be able to mess that up too badly."

Roger laughed out loud. "Well, actually, I have a surprise for you." He pushed aside the red-and-gold drapes, and in strode Desmond.

The ladies collectively gasped, and after a brief hesitation they all began talking at once. Roger and Desmond just grinned, listening to the cacophony of voices as each woman tried to out-shout the other. Finally, Roger held up his hands, asking for silence.

"One at a time, please." He winked at them.

"What are you doing here?" croaked Bella. "Are you back for good?"

"Actually, I was hoping you ladies would show up today," said Desmond. "So I snuck in the back door wanting to say a proper goodbye to you all … and maybe cook you one more breakfast … a sort of going-away gift."

"But what about Julien?" asked Ruth. "Won't he mind?"

"Are you kidding?" said Desmond. "The little cockroach hates it here. Feels unappreciated, he says. Wants to go back to

California with the rest of his surfing buddies."

"Well, if you're cooking, let's get some menus out!" shouted Bella banging her fists on the table with a celebratory thump. "I'm starving!"

"Me, too!" said Estelle, waving her arms and knocking over a glass of water.

Ruth made a quick dive and caught the glass before it tumbled onto the floor. Helen and Roger grabbed fistfuls of paper napkins and quickly mopped up.

"No need for menus this morning, ladies. Today, you're getting the house special. Breakfast is on me!"

Desmond flashed his toothy white grin and slipped back into the kitchen, while Roger got the ladies squared away with coffee, tea, small crescent breakfast rolls, three flavors of syrup, a dozen or more packets of orange marmalade, and an extra-large take home bag for Estelle.

Within ten minutes, platters of food began arriving from the kitchen. Stacks of blueberry and chocolate chip pancakes, mountains of scrambled eggs, piles of home fries, and at least a pound of bacon and homemade sausage, all cooked to perfection.

The next half hour passed quickly. Helen leaned back in her chair and rubbed her belly. "I'm so full, I can hardly breathe," she sighed. "This was absolutely wonderful."

"Yes," Bella groaned. "Food orgy. I definitely ate too much. "She burped. "And my nose is dripping. Anyone got a tissue?"

Estelle dipped into her chartreuse sweater again, pulled out another lace handkerchief, this time from her left bosom, and handed it to Bella.

Bella stared at it. "I can't use this thing," she replied, holding the corner of the handkerchief tenuously between her thumb and index finger and waving it around. "It's exactly like the one we put in the casket with my grandma Hazel, right before we shoveled dirt on top of her. Anyone got a *real* tissue?" she asked, looking around.

Ruth fished inside her purple tote, retrieved a small travel packet of tissues, and tossed it across the table. Bella caught it left-handed. She removed one tissue from the small packet, blew her nose, and tossed the used tissue in the middle of the table.

"Ew! Stop that!" screeched Ginger. "I am so tired of holding my temper every time you do that! It is such a disgusting habit. Stop throwing your used tissues on the table, or I swear I'll have you evicted!"

Bella raised her eyebrows. "Evicted? Geez, Madam President, I didn't realize you were such an important person in this place." Her voice dripped with sarcasm as she lifted the used tissue from the sugar bowl and stuffed it in her pocket.

"Well, not yet." Ginger wavered. "But maybe someday ..."

"That's right," Helen snickered. "Who knows, she just might decide to buy it after our lottery winnings come in. Then she'll be able to evict you legally for recklessly endangering the health of your friends."

"Yeah!" added Ginger defiantly. "I just might just do that. After our lottery winnings come in," she repeated.

"So tell me, Estelle, if you count up all the tickets we bought last week, how much did we win?" asked Bella. "Two million? Three million?"

The ladies all turned to look at Estelle.

Estelle shrugged. "To tell the truth, I've been so upset this week, I completely forgot to check the numbers." She reached into her purse, pulled out the ten assorted tickets they had purchased the week before, and spread them out on the table. Two of them landed in a puddle of melted butter and slid onto her lap.

"Well, did you at least save the newspaper clipping with the winning numbers?" asked Ruth.

Estelle pouted and bit her lower lip. She shook her head, *no*.

"Easy come, easy go," snorted Bella while reaching for the last of the chocolate chip pancakes. "Then I guess Miss Ginger does not have the authority to throw me out of here quite yet." She cackled smugly.

"Oh yeah, well, you just wait a minute," said Ginger. "I'm not giving up so fast. The winning numbers have got to be online somewhere."

Ginger pushed aside the platter of scrambled eggs, mopped up some maple syrup that was on the table in front of her, and began punching in numbers on her iPhone. The phone made a ringing sound, lit up, and then died.

"Ooh." She moaned, "I think I forgot to charge the batteries last night."

Helen waved to Roger, gesturing for a coffee refill. "Honestly, I think you're all nuts," she said, pouring a large splash of half-and-half into her cup. "Estelle, with all that you've spent on various forms of lottery tickets these last couple of years, how much have you actually won?"

Roger filled up everyone's coffee, tea, and water glasses one last time. "Can I get you ladies anything else?" he asked the group.

Ginger looked up at him. "I was just wondering, have there been any offers to buy this place yet?" she asked.

"And what do we owe you for this fabulous feast?" asked Ruth.

"And do you think Desmond has any more of those cinnamon buns back there in the kitchen? I'd sure like to bring some to my Bridge Club," asked Bella.

"Since when do you have a Bridge Club?" asked Helen.

"Three dollars and ninety-two cents," replied Estelle.

"Does that include all the pennies, nickels and dimes you picked up from the sidewalk this week?" asked Ruth.

Estelle nodded.

"It must have been a good week for loose change," interjected Helen.

Ginger raised her hand and waved it in front of Roger's face. "By the way, would you happen to have any of this past week's newspapers with the winning lottery numbers in them?"

"I don't believe you actually have a Bridge Club, Bella. I bet you want to eat the cinnamon buns all by yourself later tonight," chuckled Ruth.

"Well, I might share a few with Aldon, if he's nice," Bella confessed.

"But that was only for this year," pondered Estelle. "Quite frankly, I don't remember anything much at all from last year, although I'm certain I got something."

"I was pretty good at Bridge once," mused Helen, "a long time ago."

"*Yes!*" shouted Roger, silencing them all. Then he turned and left the room.

"What did he say?" asked Estelle.

"He said 'yes'," repeated Helen.

"To what?" asked Ginger.

Ruth scratched her head. "I have no idea."

Five minutes later, Roger returned. He pointed an accusing finger at each lady in turn.

"Helen, no. Ruth, nothing. Bella, Desmond says they'll be ready in five minutes. Estelle, you didn't ask, but he's also packing up a batch of those little crescent rolls you like. And Ginger, here's what I could find." He dropped a stack of old newspapers on the table and ran out of the room before the ladies could ask for anything else.

"I think we finally frightened him," said Ruth after the red-

and-gold drapes stopped swaying.

The ladies looked at each other and laughed.

"He'll get over it," said Helen. "What's next?"

"Time to check our numbers," said Ginger, rubbing the new hive blossoming on her neck. "Let's clear this table. I'm feeling lucky today."

The ladies stacked all the used plates and silverware in one corner of the table and wiped the remaining space with the leftover red cloth napkins. Ruth squirted hand sanitizer onto Estelle's lace handkerchief and gently rinsed off all ten lottery tickets, ridding them of the extra maple syrup and butter they seemed to have acquired during breakfast.

Helen took hold of the tickets. Her brow furrowed. "Should we line them up by size, date, or value?" she asked the group.

"Oh, for God's sake," groaned Bella. "Who cares?"

"Value," insisted Ginger. "Definitely by value. Let's start with the cheapest ones first and work our way up to the million-dollar ones last."

Ruth smiled at Helen. "You heard Madam President. Deal away."

"Can we wait just one more minute before we start this?" asked Estelle.

"Now what?" groaned Bella.

Estelle leaned over and whispered to the group, "I've got to go pee again. I promise, it'll only take me a second."

The other four ladies leaned back and watched Estelle's curly white ringlets bob up and down as she pried herself out of her chair and headed for the restroom across the hall.

Meanwhile, Helen sorted the ten tickets according to value and laid them out on the table, and Ginger flipped the newspaper open to the one page she could find containing lottery information.

Five minutes later Estelle scooched back into her chair. "So what do we have?" she asked.

"We have four different categories of tickets: three Scratch-its, four Oregon Quick Picks, two Mega Millions, and one Power Ball," said Helen. "I lined up each of the four categories according to the value of the prize money and put them in size place."

"Of course you did," said Bella. "So, which goes first?"

"The Scratch-its," answered Helen. "We have three different kinds. The smallest is this Wheel of Fortune ticket. Estelle, why don't you scratch off these bars and see if we won anything."

Estelle took a dime from her purse and scratched off the designated spots.

"Nope. Nothing," she said.

Ginger did the same with the Aces & 8s ticket, as did Bella with the Red Hot Riches ticket, neither of which produced even a penny in prizes.

"Okay," said Helen. "Moving on to the Oregon Quick Picks. We have four of those dollar ones. If I read out the numbers, Ginger, can you check them against the winning numbers in the newspaper?"

Ginger nodded.

"I'm sure we will win something," said Estelle. "Everyone does. Even if it is only another ticket for a free game."

Helen read out all the numbers for each of the four cards. Ginger checked them in the paper.

"Well?" asked Ruth.

"Nothing," said Ginger.

"Wait a minute," said Helen, squinting at the fine print. "This last one says we won one free dollar ticket, which we can pick up at the store where we bought the original."

"Whoop-de-do," whispered Ginger.

"Waste of time," groaned Bella.

"Seven down, three to go," said Ruth, ignoring her friend.

"These are for the big prize money," Ginger sang. "Don't lose faith. We may get something yet."

"Okay," said Ginger, "Estelle, you picked these numbers, so why don't you read them out to me, and I'll check them against the winning numbers. Let's hope that at least some of them match."

Helen handed the three remaining tickets to Estelle.

Estelle took the tickets. "Which one should I start with?"

"Start with one of the Mega Millions tickets," said Ginger.

Ruth interrupted. "I've never done lottery tickets before. How does this work?"

A machine picks five numbered white balls and one numbered Mega Ball out of a big pile. If the numbers we picked correspond to the numbers the machine picked, we win," said

Helen.

"So read out our numbers already, and let's see if any match," Ginger said to Estelle.

Estelle read "Five, twelve, thirteen, fifteen, eighteen, and twenty."

"So?" asked Bella.

"Nothing," mumbled Ginger.

"Not even one number matched?" asked Ruth.

Ginger shook her head no.

"What kind of meshugeneh numbers did you pick that we can't even get one right?" asked Bella.

"They weren't meshugeneh numbers," Estelle protested. "I chose the name Morton and converted each of the letters to a number." Estelle rubbed her forehead. "But I do have to confess I cheated a bit. You see, Morton is really spelled with two *o's*. But since I couldn't use *o* twice, I spelled Morton with an *e* this time. Maybe that was the problem."

"Who is Morton?" asked Helen, eyebrows raised and furrowed into one long, wavy line across her brow.

"Her Chihuahua," answered Ruth.

Roger poked his head through the drapes. "You ladies doing okay?" he asked.

"As well as can be expected for a bunch of crazy ladies," shouted Ginger.

"We're taking the scenic route to the poor house," groaned Helen.

"We're fine," said Ruth.

Roger disappeared.

"Can we please move onto the next Mega Millions card, before I die of old age?" asked Bella.

Estelle read out, "One …"

"We have a one!" shouted Ginger.

"How much did we win?" asked Bella.

"Nothing yet," said Helen. "Keep going, Estelle."

Estelle read out, "Seven …"

"We have a seven!" shouted Ginger. "Keep going."

Estelle read out, "Nine …"

"We have a nine, which is also the Mega Ball number!" shouted Ginger.

Estelle read out, "Twelve, fifteen, eighteen."

Silence.

"So?" asked Ruth.

"Nope. No twelve, fifteen, or eighteen," said a deflated Ginger.

"Are you sure?" asked Helen.

"I'm sure," said Ginger.

Bella grabbed the paper from Ginger's hands. "So how much did we win for two regular balls and a Mega Ball?

Helen pouted.

"Five bucks ... before taxes."

"That's it?" Helen nodded. "I'm not going to say I told you so, but—I told you so.

"Complete waste of time," muttered Bella, reaching for another tissue.

"I'm just curious, Estelle. Did you use a Chihuahua name for this Mega Millions ticket also?" asked Ginger.

"Yes," said Estelle, shyly. "I used Gloria. The name of my girl Chihuahua."

"Only one left," said Helen. "Please tell me you didn't use your cat for our Power Ball ticket."

"Daisy? No, I didn't," said Estelle. "I mean, I would have, but Daisy only has five letters and we needed six. So I picked something else really special, but I'm not going to tell you, because that would be bad luck."

"Is there any other kind?" murmured Helen.

The ladies sighed.

"Okay, everybody, this is The Power Ball. Our last try for fame and fortune," said Ginger." She turned to Ruth. "It works the same as the last two, except you get five white balls and one red one."

"And how much can you win in this one?" Bella asked.

"Usually a lot," Helen answered. "But someone won the jackpot a couple of weeks ago, so it's only up to about $50 million now."

Ruth yawned. "Just read out the numbers, Estelle, so that we can all go home. It's getting late, and I promised Gordon I would go with him to the Expo Center to look at gardening stuff."

"Okay," said Estelle. "You ready, Ginger?"

"I'm ready," said Ginger. "Go for it."

Estelle brought the ticket close to her face and in one breath read "One, four, five, fourteen, nineteen, twenty."

"Great reading. So what does the paper say?" asked Ruth.

Ginger read the numbers out loud. "One, four, five, fourteen, nineteen, twenty." She blinked, then looked up at her friends.

"Read your numbers again, Estelle," directed Ruth, who was suddenly wide awake.

"One, four, five, fourteen, nineteen, twenty."

"And yours again, Ginger."

"One, four, five, fourteen, nineteen, twenty."

Silence.

"You're joking, right?" said Ruth.

Ginger shook her head from side to side.

"You know this is statistically impossible," Helen stated. She pulled the paper out of Ginger's hands and stared at the line of printed numbers. Her heart began to pound.

Estelle looked at her friends. A huge smile lit her face. "I told you I picked a very special name this time,"

"What name?" asked Ruth.

"Dante's, of course! It had to work! I don't know why I didn't think of it sooner."

Bella stood up and stared over Helen's shoulder. "Holy shit!" she shrieked.

The ladies immediately dove into the rest of the pile of newspapers but could not find any other confirming lottery results in either of the two remaining local weeklies.

"I don't believe it," said Ruth.

"Oh my God!" screeched Helen. "I think we won the lottery!" She grabbed one of the discarded newspapers and began fanning herself.

Bella began wheezing. She sat down in her chair, leaned back, and began taking deep breaths. "I think I'm having a heart attack," she squeaked, clutching her chest. "Someone call 911."

"Not now!" Ginger snapped, "We're too busy getting rich!"

CHAPTER 36 — ALTERATIONS
AND DEPARTURES

"Could this be real?" asked Ruth. "I mean, really real?"

"I'm afraid to say it out loud, but at first glance seems so," Helen whispered, checking the numbers one more time.

"Before we all go completely bonkers, we need to verify these numbers on the internet," said Ginger. "Does anyone have a phone that works?"

Ruth dug into her purple tote and tossed her phone to Ginger, whose hands were shaking so hard she was unable to use it. She tossed it back to Ruth and began screaming at the top of her lungs. "We're millionaires!!!"

"Shh!" shouted Ruth.

"Why, shh?" asked Ginger. "I was just warming up!"

"Because ... Well, just because. I just know we have to be quiet about this until we get a plan of action."

"Plan of action?" questioned Bella, suddenly revived. "There's only one plan of action. Three easy steps: turn in the ticket, get the cash, and spend it!"

Estelle looked up just as Roger and Desmond plowed through the red-and-gold drapes.

"We heard screaming," said Roger. "Are you ladies okay?"

"We won the lottery!" screamed Ginger. "We're rich!"

Ruth reached over and pinched Ginger's arm.

"Ouch! What did you do that for?"

"I told you. You're supposed to keep quiet about this until we find out if this is real. There are way too many scams out there, and we've got to find out if this is legitimate."

Ginger looked up at the guys, who stood frozen in place. "Okay, don't say anything," she directed. Turning toward Ruth, she flatly stated, "There. We're good." Then she started screaming again and running around the room.

Ruth rolled her eyes.

The rest of the ladies continued to jabber loudly until Estelle picked up the napkin dispenser and slammed it down on the table. Dozens of napkins fluttered like white wings landing on the floor. Ginger, Ruth, Helen, and Bella stopped talking and stared at her.

"Now that I have your attention," Estelle said to the silenced group, "I know I didn't have any cash last week, and you ladies helped pick out and buy these lottery tickets. But the truth is, only one person actually put their name on the winning ticket and that was me." She looked around, "So, win or lose, officially this is *my* ticket."

She stared at Roger and Desmond, who remained in the doorway, eyes bulging, silent as stone.

Estelle turned to her friends. "We are all blessed women. We have husbands who love us … for better or worse. We have beautiful families, homes, food, and friends. We may not have *everything* we want, but we certainly have enough to survive and flourish. So, as far as this money is concerned, our first order of business has to be taking care of those whose lives are not quite as secure as ours."

"What are you talking about, Estelle?" interjected Ruth.

"I am saying that I am not going to share a single dime of these winnings with you ladies unless, right off the top, we agree to buy this damn place and give Roger and Desmond back their jobs."

Silence.

"Yes!" screamed Ginger, jumping to her feet and pumping her fists in the air.

"Definitely, yes," repeated Ruth, nodding her head.

Helen's face curled into a hesitant smile. "I'm in," she said, barely above a whisper as her brain calculated percentages. "Assuming this whole lottery thing isn't just a fraud."

Bella stared at Desmond. "Well, I'm not so sure. Can we have cinnamon buns on the menu every day?"

"Every day," replied Desmond, his eyes reflective pools of disbelief.

"And wine and lottery tickets restored?"

"Sounds good to me," he stuttered hesitantly.

"Okay, then I'm in, too."

Roger tried to speak, but no words came out. Estelle walked

over to the two men and put her arms around the guys as best she could.

"We're family, you know."

"You really think you won the lottery?" Roger's voice cracked.

"I can't believe I'm saying this, but it appears to be a distinct possibility," answered Ruth.

"And you would really consider buying this place?"

"Yes," answered Helen soberly, "But first, we've got to verify that this ticket is legitimate and that we really won. Then, we've got to find out how soon we can get our hands on the prize money."

"How much do you think we will each get?" asked Ruth.

"If ours is the only winning ticket, there'll be more than enough loot to buy this dump," said Bella, grinning from ear to ear.

"But we've got to make sure Mr. Cod Cakes doesn't sell it to anyone else before we collect," stated Helen. "Roger, would you know if there are any negotiations going on?"

"Not sure about negotiations, but I did hear that someone was interested," he added.

"Okay," said Ruth, "then we've got to act fast. Roger, will you get me the information on how to reach what's-his-name?"

"Easy," he grinned.

Estelle looked at her friends with bright eyes. "Good. Then as soon as we find out if everything is legit, I'll call Cod-cakes, and hopefully put down a deposit that will seal the deal toward the purchase of Dante's. And when the actual prize money comes in, you guys can pay me back. Is that okay with the rest of you?"

Ruth picked up a handful of the white napkins and placed them on the table. She scratched her head, her eyebrows furrowed. "We are talking about several hundred thousand dollars, Estelle. Where are you going to get that kind of money?"

Estelle grinned. "Remember when you ladies were visiting my new condo and we found all those $100 bills in-between the dishes?"

The group nodded.

"Well, that was just the tip of the iceberg. Nothing compared to what David, my skinflint husband, had socked away inside our mattress, and the matching recliners." Estelle beamed. "Yes. Apparently, I can afford it."

"I told you!" Bella screeched. "It was in the mattress all along!"

"Buying Dante's is one thing," said Ginger, opening a new tube of cortisone cream, "but who is going to run it?" Ginger turned toward Ruth. "I mean, you certainly made it clear that you didn't think I was qualified." She rubbed a glop of cortisone on two hives that had blossomed on her left cheek.

"Well, I nominate Roger," said Ruth. "If by some miracle all this goes through,"—she hesitated—"would you be willing to step up from head waiter to a manager, or whatever they call it? I mean, to be in charge of the whole restaurant?"

Roger nodded. "I would. Absolutely."

"Good!" said Estelle. "And Desmond, would you be willing to be our chief cook, or chef, or whatever you want to call yourself?"

Desmond's face lit up again with a great toothy grin. "Yes, ma'am!" he shouted.

"Then by the power of this investment we are about to plunge into, I now pronounce us ... a team!" shouted Ginger. And she began dancing around the tables again.

Estelle, completely ignoring Ginger's outburst, smiled her biggest smile ever. "Then it's settled. We can negotiate your raises as soon as the deal is confirmed."

"Ooh," exclaimed Bella jumping out of her chair. "Can I be the one to fire Julien?"

"Definitely," said Estelle. "But you have to wait until we actually own this place, or it won't count."

Ginger eyed Roger and Desmond. "We've still got a ton of stuff to figure out, but I'm hoping you guys might be able to scrounge up a bottle or two of whatever alcohol you have secretly stashed in the back cupboard so that we can make a toast."

Roger and Desmond exchanged secretive glances. "How does champagne sound?" asked Roger.

"Wonderful!" sang Ginger. "But remember, mum's the word about this until we tell you. Otherwise, Ruth is going to kill me."

Desmond and Roger exchanged secretive glances. "I think we can do Mumm's," Desmond whispered.

"And I think I'd better call Gordon and tell him to go to the Expo Center without me," said Ruth.

"Which brings me to the next question." Helen cleared her throat. "When are we going to break the news to our husbands?" She reached across the table and took a long sip of cold coffee. "I mean, we have to tell them, right?"

"Why?" asked Bella.

"Because," said Ruth. "They're going to find out sooner or later. Might as well make it sooner."

"David probably won't remember even if I do tell him," muttered Estelle. "I'm lucky if he even remembers my name these days."

"Maybe we can all meet for brunch at my place tomorrow, and we can break it to them together, as a group," Ruth offered.

"You mean I've got to keep quiet for another twenty-four hours?" asked Ginger. "I don't know if I can do that," she whined. "It's just not in my nature."

"Then you can sleep over at my house tonight and tell Bojo all about it," Bella offered. "He doesn't speak English yet, but I'm sure he'd be happy to hear the news. If he doesn't throw up on you, that is."

"It's either that, or you can bite on a sock," said Helen.

"Aren't you supposed to bite a bullet?" asked Estelle.

"Yes, but I was trying to be polite," Helen answered.

Ginger aimed an obscene gesture at Helen and plopped back into her chair.

Helen began waving her hand, trying to get everyone's attention. "I have a name!" she called out to the group.

"Of course you do," said Bella. "It's Helen Kahn, and your husband's name is Bill."

"Not *my* name, Bella. I mean a new name for the restaurant. I think we should call this place Estelle's Hideaway." She grinned. "After all, none of this would be happening if not for Estelle and her obsession with buying all those damn lottery tickets. It's perfect. What do you all think?"

"Estelle's Hideaway certainly sounds better than Pierre's Continental Bistro," said Ruth. "But you're jumping the gun, don't you think? We don't own the restaurant yet, so I don't think we have to decide that now."

"I was also thinking that as soon as we do own this place," Helen continued, "one of the first things I'd like to do is buy a real door for this banquet room, and set fire to those damn red-and-gold drapes.

"So, we'd better make certain we have fire insurance." Estelle nodded pensively.

"And how about a paint job, for the whole place," added Bella. "Getting rid of that ugly red-and-brown stuff is tops on my list."

Ruth stood up. "Oy! Life has suddenly gotten so much more complicated!" She started biting the nail of her right index finger. "There's so much to be done, assuming that everything goes through. I'm not even sure if I know where to begin. But I do know this much … we're going to need a financial planner to deal with the prize money, and a lawyer to help us buy this place." She reached into her purple tote and pulled out a writing tablet. "Lists," she muttered. "Gotta start writing lists."

"And the menu," said Ginger, ignoring Ruth's distress. "Maybe we can have specials each day. Wouldn't that be so cool? Like Mushroom Monday."

"And Turnip Tuesday," added Estelle.

"And Wedgy Wednesday," chimed in Bella.

"Wedgy Wednesday?" exclaimed Helen. "You're all out of your minds!"

"Well," said Estelle, "technically the menu is up to Desmond. Although, I don't think he would mind if we made a few suggestions. Like, I'm certain he would love to have the recipe for my grandmother's carrot cake."

"Oh boy …" said Ruth, dropping her head in her hands. "I can't believe this is even happening, or that we are doing this. I feel a migraine coming on."

"Then let's get out of this room," suggested Helen. "Getting some fresh air will make you feel better."

The ladies left the little banquet area and made their way into the main dining room just as Roger finished pouring the first of four bottles of Mumm's Brut Corson Rouge Champagne into crystal goblets.

"I'm not even going to ask where all this came from," whispered Bella, sauntering up to the counter and reaching for a glass.

"I just thought of something," said Helen. "We are going to have to drive all the way down to the Oregon Lottery office in Salem to verify the ticket."

"You're right!" declared Estelle. "So really, we should we leave now. I know a nice motel we can stay in, and then we can be at the lottery office as soon as it opens tomorrow morning."

"Ugh," groaned Bella. "I can't go tonight. I'm babysitting for Bojo again."

"And it's Scrabble night at the senior center," said Helen. "Can we pick another day?"

"We have to. Howard and I have concert tickets tonight," said Ginger, polishing off another goblet of champagne.

"Don't look at me," added Ruth. "As it is, Gordon is going to be furious because I'm skipping out on the Expo Center. I better be home tonight."

"Okay," said Ginger, "let's table the trip for a minute. There's no rush. Some people wait weeks before coming forward. We certainly can wait a few days. Meanwhile, as all this soaks in, we can just sort of discuss some little changes we would like to put on our wish list."

"We have a wish list?" asked Estelle.'

"Apparently," answered Ruth.

In the next hour Bella made clear that she expected to replace all the small round tables with larger square ones. Estelle wanted bigger chairs with fluffy cushions. Helen wanted a complete interior makeover, including all new window treatments. Desmond hinted that a new dishwasher would be welcome. Roger said they needed more staff. And so it went.

"Hey...Does anyone know what time it is?" asked Ruth at last.

Helen checked her watch. "Almost two."

Ruth picked up her purple tote. "Well, I for one have had more than enough excitement for today. I am going home to process, and take a nap," she said, reaching for her car keys.

"Well, which is it?" asked Bella. "Are you going to process or nap?

"I process while I nap," Ruth answered sharply, polishing off her third glass of champagne.

"Me too," said Estelle, "but first, I've got to go pee again," she added as she trotted toward the restroom.

Bella burped, and giggled, and burped again. "Boy, that was good champagne," she said, smacking her lips.

"Are you ladies going to be okay driving home?" asked Roger. "You all look a little tipsy to me." He stood back and watched them sway side to side as they edged toward the front door.

"I can have some fresh coffee brewed in just a minute."

"Nope," hiccupped Ginger. "Don't want ruin a good thing."

"Don't worry about us, Roger. We'll take a few laps around the parking lot before we get in our cars," said Ruth as she headed toward the front door. "That'll sober us up."

Helen, bleary-eyed from four glasses of champagne, stopped in the outer vestibule and rubbed her hand lovingly over the lumpy red walls. "Goodbye, tomato rice soup," she whispered. "Who knows? The next time we meet, you may look more like minestrone ... or maybe even chicken gumbo."

"Come on, Helen," said Ruth, grabbing Helen by the sleeve and pulling her outside into the sunlight. "We're leaving."

"Wait for me," said Estelle, taking a pair of wrap-around sunglasses from the front pocket of her chartreuse sweater and hooking them over her face. "I've been thinking about the name of this place since Helen brought it up," she said, slowly navigating onto the sidewalk. "And if it is okay with the rest of you, I'd really like to go back to calling it Dante's Café."

"I agree." Ruth nodded, allowing Estelle to lean on her shoulder for balance. "I've always called it Dante's anyhow, regardless of what the sign said."

"But what should I do with that pretty Estelle's Hideaway sign I had made up?" asked Helen.

"You had a sign made up?" asked Ginger.

"Well, not really," Helen admitted. "Just in my head."

Bella giggled. "If you really want the perfect place to hang your Estelle's Hideaway sign, stick it in the ladies' room!" Then she took off, leading her friends on their first lap around the parking lot.

Roger and Desmond stared out the bay windows of the

restaurant and watched the five old women weave around the parked cars in the back lot.

"I told you a long time ago they were Dante's Angels," said Desmond.

"Yes, you did," said Roger, smiling broadly.

"Do you really think they are going to buy this place?"

"Well, I think they're going to try."

"And then what?" asked Desmond.

"With these old ladies, God only knows," Roger chuckled.

The two men remained by the window for the next half hour, savoring with affectionate amusement the old women's antics as they wound their way around each of the cars in the parking lot, arm-in-arm, singing and laughing, and planning a new world of tomorrows under the bright summer sky.